ELIZA BING
IS (NOT)
A STAR

Carmella Van Vleet

Holiday House 🐿 New York

Library of Congress Cataloging-in-Publication Data
Names: Van Vleet, Carmella, author.
Title: Eliza Bing is (not) a star / by Carmella Van Vleet.
Description: First Edition. | New York : Holiday House, [2018] | Sequel to: Eliza
Bing is (not) a big, fat quitter. | Summary: Eliza Bing does her best to conquer the
sixth grade, new friendships, after-school taekwondo, and a role in the school play.
Identifiers: LCCN 2017043191 | ISBN 9780823440245 (hardcover)
Subjects: | CYAC: Theater—Fiction. | Best friends—Fiction. | Friendship—Fiction.
| Taekwondo—Fiction. | Family life—Fiction. | Middle schools—Fiction.
| Schools—Fiction.
Classification: LCC PZ7.V378 Eo 2018 | DDC [Fic]—dc23 LC record
available at https://lccn.loc.gov/2017043191

ISBN: 978-0-8234-4430-4 (paperback)

For Abbey—the real-life Eliza

NEW RULE: DON'T VOLUNTEER

Master Kim once said a good martial artist focuses his or her mind on the lesson at all times. But a million cupcakes says he's never sat through Mr. Roddel's lab-safety lecture. Sorting socks would be more exciting.

Mr. R taught biology, but now that we'd been in school for a couple of weeks, both sixth-grade classes were going to do a chemistry unit and take turns using the lab. Annie was in the other biology class. We'd doubled up to get the safety talk because their class had a substitute who knew more about binomials than Bunsen burners.

Annie nudged my elbow. "Eliza," she whispered. I looked over and she pretended to fall asleep.

Annie wanted to be an actor someday, so she was always playing around like that. I didn't know what I wanted to be when I grew up. Taekwondo and making cakes were more my thing. But I faked a yawn, which made Annie yawn for real. And that made me giggle.

Zoe turned around. "Do you mind?" she snapped.

"No, I don't mind," Annie said sweetly, as if Zoe had asked if she could cut in line or something.

Annie and I started a Rules to Surviving Sixth Grade list on the second day of school. And she was breaking Rule No. 4: Don't get on Zoe Goldberg's bad side. (No. 1: Buy, don't pack. No. 2: Write your locker combo on the bottom of your shoe. And No. 3: Don't sit in the first row of Ms. Miller's class because she spits when she talks.) I appreciated Annie sticking up for me. Tony, my ex-best-friend, never laughed at me. But he never stood up for me, either.

Zoe stared at us, confused. When she finally turned back around, Annie held up four fingers just for me and grinned. I grinned back. Then Annie nodded toward Mr. Roddel to let me know we needed to pay attention. Annie liked horsing around, but she also liked getting good grades.

"Now. Since the weather will be turning chilly soon, you may want to wear scarves," Mr. Roddel said. "You'll need to leave them in your lockers. Loose clothing is dangerous when we're working with the Bunsen burners. And if you have long hair"—here Mr. R paused and eyed a kid named Matt—"you'll need to tie it back while in class as well."

Matt had long, curly hair. He never pulled it back, so his head looked like a mop. That would never fly at taekwondo class. Master Kim had long hair, too, but he wore it in a ponytail. Mine was just long enough for a stubby ponytail. It used to be longer, but I got it cut short. Mom kept asking, "Are you sure you want to do that? You can't undo it," like I was five and didn't understand how hair worked.

I did regret doing it, though. But when Annie first saw me, she said it was "Oh-my-gosh chic!" Well, actually, it came out as "Ohmygoshchic" because Annie talks really fast. She was just being nice, though. (She reminded me of

Sweet Caroline of *Sweet Caroline Cakes*, my favorite show. Caroline always says, "Be sweet to those you meet!")

Annie had called me out of the blue when I didn't show up for Orientation Day. She was excited the two of us were in the same homeroom. Last year we'd been in different classes, but we went to the same orthodontist, Dr. Ohno. I'd missed orientation because I was at the ER after I'd jumped down the stairs and bruised my coccyx. If you don't know what that is, look it up. It's embarrassing, and I'm not going to talk about it or the inflatable donut I had to sit on for a week. That was all right before my yellow-belt test. Which, FYI, I passed.

Mr. Roddel moved everyone to the back of the room, near the safety shower. He held up the eyewash bottle and showed us how to use it. We weren't supposed to rub. Just rinse for fifteen minutes and roll your eyeballs around inside your head to make sure nothing got missed. I tried to imagine how you went about rolling your eyeballs inside your head for that long. Should you make circles? Would shaking your head shake your eyeballs, too?

Mr. Roddel caught my attention and tapped his left ear. It was his way of telling me to focus. He came up with it in our "strategies for success" meeting. My parents and I have those every year with my teachers because of my ADHD. I was pretty sure having biology second-to-last period wasn't a very good strategy for success. My medicine started to wear off by then.

"So, in the exceedingly rare event that your clothes catch on fire or you spill chemicals on yourself, make your way quickly to the shower," Mr. Roddel told us. "It's important that you don't panic."

I leaned over and whispered, "Don't panic," to Annie. She gave me her best *Who me?* face, which made me want to giggle again. But I didn't. I slapped my hand over my mouth to stifle a snicker so I didn't get Mr. Roddel's attention. Middle school was going to be different. I was going to stop blurting things out and doing things without thinking in class. I was going to have a best friend who didn't ditch me (like Tony did) and I'd have my first sleepover.

"Once here"—Mr. Roddel fanned his hand over the shower base—"you'll need to . . . Hold up. Let's do and understand."

Everyone groaned because Mr. Roddel always said that. He was in love with the Confucius quote: *I hear and I forget. I see and I remember. I do and I understand.* He even had *two* posters of it on the wall.

"Who would like to volunteer?" he asked. I wanted to make up for not paying attention before, so when no one else raised their hand, I did.

"Thank you, Eliza!" Mr. Roddel said. I started to take my shoes off, but he stopped me and told us that, in an emergency, we should just get inside the shower as quickly as possible.

I stepped under the showerhead and suddenly felt silly standing there. In front of everyone. In a shower.

"Next," Mr. Roddel announced, "you will pull down on

the chain." I grabbed the air next to the chain and gave it a fake tug.

"And that's it! Gravity will do the rest. Any questions?"

No one had any, so Mr. R told me I could step out. I was in a hurry to go back to the group and forgot I was standing inside a four-inch-tall shower base.

Oomph!

My right foot banged against the edge and I stumbled forward. I reached out, both arms waving wildly as I tried to grab on to something—anything!—to keep from falling.

My left hand landed on the chain. Without thinking, I pulled myself up.

HOLY GUACAMOLE

It was raining. And not just on me.

When I'd put my weight on the shower chain, it pulled the ceiling pipe down and cracked it open. Water sprayed out in all directions. People squealed. Others shrieked. Everyone scrambled.

"Calm down and move this way!" Mr. Roddel called. But no one was really listening.

"Yeeess!" a boy said.

"Aw, man. I wish I had my phone," another boy, named Collin, said. "This would go viral!"

A girl used her folder as an umbrella. "This is a brand-new shirt!" she complained.

I backed against the wall, out of the way. It was too late, though. I was soaked. Annie was off to one side, looking damp and crossing her arms over her chest.

The commotion brought Miss Moorehouse, the history teacher from next door, running to the room. *"Should I pull the fire alarm?"* she yelled.

"No," Mr. Roddel called over the noise.

Criminy! The last thing I needed was the whole school having to evacuate because of something dumb I did.

Miss Moorehouse managed to get everyone to the front of the chem lab while Mr. Roddel called the office.

The two classes crammed together as best they could to avoid the spray. When the water began streaming across the floor, some of the girls stood on their tiptoes or on chairs. A few boys splashed each other.

"Settle down, folks," Miss Moorehouse scolded. "It's water; it won't hurt you."

"Well, technically, it can," a boy named Michael said. "About ten people drown each day." He was one of those people who always had random facts handy.

Miss Moorehouse frowned at him.

A few minutes later, the maintenance guy came waltzing in with a big wrench. He went straight to the closet in the corner of the room and turned the emergency shutoff valve.

"Awwww," some people complained. Everyone else cheered.

The place was a disaster with a capital D. Water continued to drip from the pipe and make tiny splashes in the puddles in the back of the room. The rest of the floor was covered in a shallow layer of water. There was a drain in the middle of the floor, but it was clogged by something that looked like someone's math notes. In the back, near the shower, a poster that said SAFETY RULES was a soggy mess and peeling off the wall. Some books on a nearby lab table were ruined, too.

People began shaking out their wet clothes or running their hands through damp hair. "I need a comb," someone called out. The kids with glasses grabbed tissues to dry them off.

"You better hope my shoes aren't ruined!" a girl whose name I didn't know said. "They were expensive."

"That. Was. Epic!" a boy said, and fist-bumped his friend.

"If my watch is toast, you're buying me a new one," another boy warned.

A girl complained as she wiped off the mascara running down her face.

"Great. Just great," Zoe muttered.

From all around the room, glaring, amused, and shocked eyes found me in the back.

And then Michael started slow clapping. "Nice job, Nimbus!" he said.

SQUISHED, SQUASHED

*N*imbus.

    I got the joke right away. And since we'd talked about weather in class last week, apparently so did lots of other people.

Nimbus clouds were rain clouds.

My face and chest were hot with shame, but the rest of me shivered from the cold water. I hunched my shoulders and wished I could shrink enough to disappear down the drain. I'd been called Spaz and a weirdo before. And last year, people called me Every Day Eliza because sometimes I wore the same outfit for a few days in a row when I found a comfortable one. But nimbus clouds were gray and depressing and ruined people's day.

"There will be no name-calling," Miss Moorehouse announced over the laughter.

There were about a dozen people who were wet. Including Zoe (ugh) and her friend Ava. Mr. Roddel handed each of us a long section of paper towels as we walked out the door. "The office is expecting you," he told us. "Be quiet in the halls."

Because I'd been right under the broken pipe, I got the worst of it. My tennis shoes *squish squish squished* down the hall. I stopped and yanked them off. But then I had to move more slowly to avoid slipping. Peach pits! Even my socks were soaked.

"Want me to hang back with you?" Annie asked. She

still had her arms crossed, but now she had her notebook in front of her, too.

"That's okay," I said.

"I don't mind."

"I'll meet you there," I told her.

"Are you sure?"

I nodded. I figured Annie would wait anyway, but she turned around and kept going down the hall. I didn't blame her. All I wanted to do was get out of my cold, wet clothes as quickly as possible, too.

Right outside the front office was the Citizens of the Month board. One person from each grade was nominated by teachers. Annie had been picked for September, so her picture and a list of her favorite things were hanging up. Favorite food: cupcakes. Favorite color: green. Favorite subject: language arts.

After this, I bet I could go the entire three years of middle school and never be chosen as a Citizen of the Month.

When I got to the office, the rest of the kids from class were crammed around the secretary's desk. I stood next to Annie. "So," I said. "What are we supposed to do?"

"We're still trying to figure that out," she said.

"I'm sorry you got wet," I told her.

"It's okay. It's not like you did it on purpose."

Man. I hoped the principal knew it was just an accident, too. And I hoped the school had insurance for broken pipes and stuff like that. Mom said that we'd used a lot of our savings to pay for Dad's tuition.

Even though I was the soggiest, I decided to go last. (It was my fault everyone was there, after all.) We had to leave our cell phones in our lockers during the day, so we took turns sharing the two office phones.

The dampest kids called home. The less damp kids were sent to the restrooms to see if they could dry off using the hand dryers. Others went through the Lost and Found box to see if there was something they could borrow.

I turned to Annie. "Did your homework get wet?" I asked her. "You can use the last bit of my paper towel."

Annie hugged her notebook closer to her chest. "No. I'll wipe it off later."

"Okay."

When one of the secretary's phones opened up, Annie called home. "I'm going to run to my locker before the bell rings," Annie told the secretary. "My mom's on her way."

"She'll have to sign you out," the secretary reminded her. "So come back. Don't just leave."

Annie ducked out of the office without so much as a glance my way. Was she mad at me? She'd told me she knew breaking the pipe was just an accident. I was in the middle of thinking of what to say to her when a commotion squashed my thoughts.

"I'm not wearing somebody else's old clothes." It was Zoe.

"Me neither," Ava said.

The secretary tried to tell them that it was better than being wet, but they kept complaining. The secretary ended up opening the Pioneer Post (the fancy name of our school supplies store) just so Zoe and Ava could buy some spirit wear.

"You can pay for them tomorrow," the secretary told Zoe.

But Zoe said, "Oh, no. I got it," and pulled out her wallet. She counted out three twenty-dollar bills to pay for the two pairs of sweatpants and matching tie-dye T-shirts. Smoked salmon! The only things I had in *my* wallet were my student ID and a card with emergency numbers.

Zoe and Ava got permission to change into their new clothes in the nurse's clinic.

That left just me.

DRIP DRY

The secretary pushed the phone in my direction. "Here. You can call someone about bringing you a new outfit." I tried Mom first.

"How on earth did you get all wet?" she asked.

I gave her the mini version of what had happened. She sighed. "Eliza, I'm sorry but I just can't leave work. We're swamped." Mom's a nurse and I could hear the usual beeps and bustle of the ER in the background. "Can you ask Dad?" she said.

I tried, but Dad was no help, either. "Sorry, kiddo. I'm

literally walking into my exam. You'll figure this out. I have faith in you."

"I have faith in you" was Dad Code for "You're on your own!" Since Mom went back to work full-time and he went back to college to become a teacher, Dad loved saying this almost as much as Mr. Roddel loved saying "Let's do and understand." I wondered if Dad would put posters up in his future classroom.

"Any luck?" the secretary asked me when I handed back the phone. I shook my head and tried to ignore the fact that doing so made my hair drip.

The secretary frowned and then started going through the Lost and Found box. "What about these?" she asked, holding up an itchy-looking sweater and a pair of purple leggings.

Nope on a rope. I didn't care how wet I was, I was not wearing those. It's not that I'm stuck-up like Zoe and Ava. But I *am* very particular about my clothes. I hate tight things. And itchy things. After Master Kim first gave me my *dobok* over the summer, I made Dad wash it a billion times because it felt like paper.

"I don't suppose you have a change of clothes in your locker?" the secretary asked me. I didn't.

"Well. What are we going to do with you? It's not like you can stand there and drip dry."

WHAT WE DID
WITH ME

The "good" news was I realized I did have a change of clothes. The bad news was they were my gym clothes. I had to go the locker room and put on my navy-blue tee and baggy black shorts. Thankfully they didn't smell too bad. (I checked.)

I dried my socks under the hand dryer in the bathroom, and afterward I put my wet clothes in the plastic bag the secretary gave me.

When I got back to the office, there was no sign of Annie. I'd text her later. I just got a new cell phone. (I lost my old one.) It was the cheapest Dad could find and I wasn't supposed to text unless it was an emergency because texting cost extra. But your best friend maybe being mad at you was an emergency.

"Well now!" the secretary declared cheerfully as she handed me a late pass for my next class. "Crisis averted!"

I wasn't sure what her definition of "averted" was, but I bet it wasn't the same as mine.

ANOTHER LESSON
ABOUT WATER

Since Mom was still working and Sam was at marching-band practice, it was only me and Dad for dinner. This wasn't surprising but it did make me a little sad. Not the being-with-my-dad part. I liked that. It just seemed my family was rarely all in the same place at the same time anymore. And if we were, it wasn't for long.

Dad brought home a pizza. He said the principal called and said what happened was just an unfortunate accident, and she was just glad everyone was okay. That was a relief. But Annie hadn't answered the text I'd sent after school. So maybe it was too early to say *everything* was okay.

Dad and I chomped down a couple of slices of pepperoni, and we made it to the community center with a few minutes to spare.

Taekwondo was practically the only place I was on time for. Which is kind of funny because the class wasn't even my idea. At first, I really wanted to take Sweet Caroline's cake-decorating class with Tony. Tony's family owned a bakery and Tony and I planned to open up our own shop someday. But Mom and Dad said no because money was tight. So when Sam dropped out of the taekwondo class that was already paid for, I struck a deal with them. If I took the class and stuck with it for the whole summer, they'd let me take the cake class in the fall. They thought I'd quit. But that's another story.

At exactly seven o'clock, Master Kim walked in and strode to the front of the room. If you saw him on the street, he probably wouldn't seem scary. But in class, Master Kim commanded your attention. His shoulders were wide and his hands looked like they could chop down a tree.

"Class, *jong yul!*" Master Kim called. "Line up!"

At my very first class, I was clueless. There were so many Korean words! And I had no idea where I was even supposed to stand. But I figured out that the highest-ranked belts lined up in the front row. The order went from right to left. (Which took some getting used to.) The black-belt helpers stood in the very back of the room, by themselves. My class was a beginner class, so the highest rank was an orange belt. I was a yellow belt, one step up from beginner, which meant I was in the last row. Sophia, the younger white belt next to me, looked nervous, so I gave her a quick smile.

At the start of every class, we did a meditation. We were supposed to sit with our legs crossed, close our eyes, and focus on our breathing. I couldn't concentrate. I kept thinking about having to walk around in my gym clothes. (An eighth grader in my last period said, "Hey, stupid. You're supposed to change after gym!") And I kept thinking about the mess I'd made, and all the people who got wet and had to go to the office. Including Annie. And how Michael had called me Nimbus.

There was no name-calling at taekwondo. The

number one rule was to respect each other at all times. There were other rules, too. Like saying "Yes, sir" and "Yes, ma'am." And bowing when you walked into the room. And before you walked out. Or bowing when you saw a black belt. Or bowing when you started working with your partner. Or when someone handed you a kicking paddle. (There was *lots* of bowing!)

"You may open your eyes," Master Kim called out. "*Yursit!*" The class stood. I always thought it was cool that a word with "sit" in it actually meant "stand up."

An orange belt bowed us in to begin training. "Class, *charyut*, attention. *Sabumnim kyoonyae.*" (This last part meant "Bow to the instructor.")

After warm-ups, Master Kim announced we were going to practice our self-defense requirements. I was working toward my gold belt, and the test was the second week of November. At my yellow-belt test, I got a Spirit Award patch for sticking with it even though I was hurt. Master Kim didn't give away awards often, so I didn't expect one for the coming test. But I still wanted to do well.

We worked on our defenses against a shove. I partnered up with Sophia. I remembered what it felt like to be a new, confused white belt, so I was kinda looking out for her. She was a couple of years younger, but we were around the same height.

"Ready?" she asked, standing about six feet away.

I gave a quick *kihap*, or spirit yell, to signal that I was. ("*Huuup!*") And then she charged at me with her hands out in front of her. I was supposed to put my own hands up in front of my body and then pivot and turn, like I was a door being opened. But she was moving too fast, and—

Pow-za!

I only sort of managed to get out of her way. Thankfully, neither of us was hurt. Not like the time I didn't get out of the way and a boy named Mark accidentally punched me in the mouth. That was the first time Madison said something nice to me, though. Madison was in my summer class. I thought she was mean and the person who started the Every Day Eliza nickname. But it turned out she wasn't. She was actually really nice. (FYI: Your brain doesn't always tell you the truth.) Madison moved to a different class after our test.

Now Sophia looked worried she'd done something wrong. "Don't worry. It's my fault," I told her. "When someone's about to plow into me, I should move!" We both laughed.

Master Kim walked over. "Do the technique again," he said to me. "But this time move *with* her."

I stared at him. Master Kim had a habit of saying Yoda-ish things like this. I guess he could tell I wasn't getting it. He called, *"Koomahn,"* which means "stop," to the rest of the class and turned my confusion into a whole class lesson. He did this a lot. But to everyone, not just me. So I didn't feel too bad.

"There is a natural balance to everything in the universe," he said. "An action and a reaction, a push and a pull. See that flag?" Master Kim pointed to the wall. On the South Korean flag, there was a circle divided in half by a line that looked kind of like an S. Half of the circle was red and the other half was blue.

"That is the symbol for yin-yang," Master Kim explained. "It represents how opposite forces exist together. Good and bad. Heaven and earth. Fire and water. Now, when someone is attacking you, you can use your opponent's momentum to your advantage. Watch."

Master Kim asked an orange belt to run at him as fast as he could. At the last second, Master Kim simply turned his body out of the way and the orange belt ran past him. "Flow *with* your opponent's energy. Be like the water, not the rock in the stream."

Master Kim had everyone take turns being the shover and the shov-ee for a few more minutes. Sophia and I plowed into each other again a couple of times.

I should be better at being water, I thought. I had plenty of practice being all wet this afternoon.

BBF

The first thing I did when I got out of class was check my phone.

No messages from Annie.

"Hey, kiddo. Mind if we stop at the store?" Dad asked when we were a few minutes from home. "We need eggs." What he really meant was he'd forgotten to buy them on Saturday. Dad was like me in the attention department.

I shook my head. And then peeked at my phone

again. Sixty-three percent battery, three service bars. And zero texts.

Was Annie embarrassed by what happened? Maybe she didn't want to be friends anymore because she thought I really was some nimbus cloud that would follow her around and ruin everything. I tried to shove the thought aside, but just like Sophia, it kept plowing into me. I needed a distraction.

"Can I check out the nail polish?" I asked Dad when we walked into the store. Mom usually made me stay with her because she's always in and out super fast when she goes shopping. Dad takes forever.

"Sure," he said. We agreed on a meeting place and time and headed in opposite directions.

There were rows and rows of nail polish. In all kinds of colors. I liked reading their names: Are You Grape Jelly?, Scaredy Cat Black, Espresso Yourself, Little Blue Peep, Lime Time, Roses and Toes are Red. And my favorite, Sweet Mermaid Tales (which was a pretty teal).

I opened the bottle of Sweet Mermaid Tales and tried it out on my thumb. I had money at home to buy it, but I was sure Dad would say no if I asked for a loan. I'd only recently been allowed to start using nail polish again. (Over the summer, there was a nail polish incident that involved an unfortunate spill, paper towels, and a clogged toilet.)

I checked my phone for the billionth time and headed over to meet Dad. Annie still hadn't responded to my text.

I didn't know what I'd do if Annie stopped being

my friend. I really liked hanging out with her. She was thoughtful. For example, she carried extra pens in case I needed one. And when we both had bad days, she'd let me complain first. She was funny and smart, too. Plus, we had tons of stuff in common. To begin with, we both liked peanut butter toast and hated the feeling of dry sand. And we both had dogs whose names started with B, Bingo (hers) and Bear (mine).

Everyone at school had a best friend or a group to hang out with. Everyone had their spot in the cafeteria. Annie would be fine without me. People liked her. But if she ditched me, I'd probably never find another friend. Or at least a new *best* friend. And then seventh grade and eighth grade would come, and I'd still be friendless. I'd probably have to beg my parents to let me go to a different high school to start over. Maybe I could change my name. . . .

"Eliza," Dad said, coming up alongside me and interrupting my thoughts. "You ready?" I noticed he had the eggs—along with a basketful of other stuff.

The two of us got in line. I couldn't stand looking at my blank phone anymore, so I read the magazine covers while we waited.

The ones in our lane were either gossip or news or what Mom called "DHW's." Those were magazines, Mom once explained, that always had stories about desserts, hair styles, or weight-loss fads.

I checked out one (it had a picture of chocolate cake).

On the cover was a headline: HOW GOOD A FRIEND ARE YOU? TAKE OUR QUIZ.

I thought I was a pretty good friend. After all, when Tony went off to the cake class without me, I tried to be understanding. But then he didn't invite me to his birthday party. And I always tried to make Annie laugh. We were writing a Rules to Surviving Sixth Grade list together. But I'd also gotten her wet and possibly ruined her reputation because she was friends with the girl who flooded the chem lab.

My chest hurt.

At our first middle-school assembly, the counselor had talked about how to make friends. She said, "To make a friend, you have to be a friend." It made sense.

I bet best friends worked the same way. If I wanted Annie to stay my best friend, I had to be her best friend, too.

Dad started unloading the basket onto the belt. "Shoot. Can you get that?" he asked, pointing to the box he dropped.

I leaned down to retrieve the cookies. At the same time, someone knocked into the candy rack from the other side and a pack of bubble gum fell right on my head. It wasn't Newton's apple, but I suddenly had an idea.

I wasn't just going to be a *good* best friend, I was going to the *best* best friend ever. If I did that, Annie would want to stick around.

Sweet Mermaid Tales, I had a plan.

Operation BBF was on!

THE NEXT DAY

Annie had Student Council meetings on Thursday mornings, so she wasn't in homeroom.

I didn't see her in the halls all morning, either. By the time lunch came around, my stomach felt like it did that one time when I accidentally made frosting with old shortening.

The two of us usually met up after we'd gotten our trays. I got to our table first and wondered if I'd be sitting there alone. I didn't think I could deal with the meat loaf. So instead, I started tearing up my napkin.

"Sorry about not texting you back," Annie said, suddenly plunking her tray down across from me. I was so relieved to see her that I almost tossed the napkin pieces like confetti.

"Mo-mo took away my phone for the night because I forgot to take out the trash. I didn't get your text till this morning." Mo-mo was one of Annie's moms.

"It's okay," I told her.

Annie started eating and I found my appetite, too.

"I was worried when you didn't text me back," I admitted. "You seemed a little mad yesterday."

Annie frowned. "Well, I kinda was. But mostly I was just worried"—she leaned in closer—"that everyone could see through my shirt."

"Oh!" I said. "That makes sense." And it did. I always made sure to wear white underwear on days I had taekwondo because you could sorta see through my *dobok* pants.

"If it makes you feel better," I told Annie, "I don't think you could." I didn't know if that was actually true, but I wanted to help.

She smiled. "Thanks. Sorry I didn't stick around. All I wanted to do was go home and change as fast as possible."

Whoa. I'd embarrassed her, and here she was apologizing *to me*.

"What did you end up doing?" she asked. I told her about the gym clothes and she winced.

Annie pulled out the Rules to Surviving Sixth Grade notebook and opened it on the table. "We should add 'Keep a change of clothes at school' to the list," she said.

I laughed and nodded. She carefully wrote it down. Annie was in charge of writing the rules because, first of all, the list was her idea. And second, her handwriting was neater than mine.

"So, switching channels," Annie said after she'd closed the notebook. "Play auditions start next Tuesday." (She got that "switching channels" thing from me.)

I looked at her. She'd been trying to talk me into going with her for the last two weeks. "Come on. Pleeease? It'll be fun," she said. "I promise."

When I didn't say anything, Annie frowned.

Picnic ants! This was the perfect chance to set Operation BBF into motion and I was already messing it up. Like salt instead of sugar in a recipe. But I'd never been onstage. What if I did something embarrassing in front of an entire audience? A classroom had been bad enough.

Annie and I noticed at the exact same time that people were standing beside our table. It was Collin, the boy who wanted make a viral video yesterday, and a few of his friends.

"Yo. What's the weather forecast, Nimbus? Chance of rain today?" Collin said. He and his friends cracked up and high-fived. I remembered Master Kim's lesson about being like water and not the rock, and decided to go with the flow. But Annie grabbed her pencil and opened our notebook to the very back page.

"So. What are your names again?" she asked with the pencil poised over the blank sheet of paper.

"Why?" one of the boys wanted to know.

Annie smiled sweetly. "No reason."

The boys looked at each other and then decided to just keep moving.

Annie turned her attention back to me. "Don't listen to them. You are not a rain cloud. In fact, you're the opposite of a rain cloud," she said, her voice rising dramatically and her hands gesturing wildly. "You're one of those giant, fluffy clouds on sunny days. The ones that look like bunnies or ice cream cones."

"Thanks!" I laughed.

"How can you be so calm about those jerks?" she asked.

I shrugged. Annie didn't take taekwondo, so it was hard to explain.

"Doesn't it bother you?"

It did. A lot. Names were like assigned seats—something you wouldn't have picked but were usually stuck with anyway.

"Yeah," I admitted. "It bothers me. But it's better to just ignore them."

"Well, you'd never know you were upset. You've got a great poker face!" Annie said. "I'm serious. You have to come to the auditions with me. Being able to keep your composure is, like, the number one skill for actors."

She was being so nice. And she'd been so forgiving about the whole getting-her-wet-and-embarrassing-her thing. My plan to be the best best friend ever was off to a disastrous start all because I was too chicken to be onstage.

Annie tried again. "It'll be an adventure," she said.

I wasn't convinced. But then I thought about how Tony had started to do other things without me. Would Annie stop being my friend if we didn't like the same things? On the other hand, the thought of auditioning . . .

"I'm too busy," I told her.

"No, you're not."

She had me there. I'd been hoping I could take Sweet Caroline's fall cake-decorating class, but I didn't have a way to get there and back. Mom had to work extra shifts. And Dad had added more classes this semester. Luckily Sam had a girlfriend with a driver's license and a car to give him rides home after band practice. Plus, the cake class cost money and, as Mom and Dad liked to remind us, "Money still doesn't grow on trees."

Annie didn't give up. "But we'll make so many new friends. For real," she said. "Plus, you're a natural, Eliza."

"You're just saying that."

"I'm not!" Annie insisted. She lowered her eyes and got quiet. "And, truth is, I also don't want to go by myself."

Something jabbed at my heart.

What would a best friend do?

STEP 1 OF OPERATION BBF

Okay. I'm in!"

DUUUUH

It was past dinnertime. Mom and Dad were arguing in the kitchen.

"I'm sorry. I forgot," Dad said. "I was running late this morning. Why didn't *you* take out something last night?"

"Why is dinner always my responsibility?" Mom responded.

I turned around and headed to the living room. I didn't like it when Mom and Dad raised their voices like that. Especially about something as dumb as dinner. I'd totally eat cereal three times a day if they'd let me. The kind that tasted like cookies was my favorite. It's too bad there isn't a tiny cupcake-shaped one. I'd eat that three times a day, too.

Since dinner was obviously going to take a while, I decided to watch TV. Sam was stretched out on the couch. "What up, E?"

I scowled in my brother's direction. Since he turned sixteen, he'd started calling everyone by their first initial all the time. He even called Mom and Dad "M" and "D." It was super annoying, but Mom said it was a phase.

"Is dinner ready?" Sam asked.

I shoved his feet off the end of the couch and plopped down. "No," I told him. "Wanna watch *Family Feud?*"

He shrugged. "Sure."

I clapped, pretending to be all excited, and said, "Good answer, good answer!" He grinned and grabbed the remote.

"We surveyed one hundred people," the host read from his card. "The top eight answers are on the board. Name something a dog might do that embarrasses its owner."

"*Sniff things!*" Sam yelled at the TV.

"*Pee on the floor!*" I said at the same time.

"Sniff things" was the number one answer.

"Ha!" Sam said to me. "In your face." I didn't mind. He wasn't really being mean. Sam was actually pretty cool most of the time. He was the one who helped me after I fell down the stairs and bruised my tailbone. And while I was at the ER, he cleaned up the mess I'd left.

One of the contestants on the show answered, "Coughs up a fur ball."

The rest of her family clapped and said, "Good answer! Good answer!"

Bear put her tiny poodle paws on the screen and barked. Even she knew that answer was silly.

Sam and I raised our arms into X's. *"Dumb answer! Dumb answer!"* we yelled at the television. Sure enough, a giant red X appeared on the screen and the buzzer sounded. I always thought it sounded like it was saying *Duuuuh!*

Sam was ahead three correct answers to my two when his phone pinged.

The goofy grin on his face told me it was Megan, his girlfriend. We hadn't officially met her yet, but Mom knew her because Megan was in the marching band, too. Mom was the band nurse on game nights and field trips.

Sam's thumbs texted a quick reply. He stared at the phone, waiting for a response. A few seconds later, he grinned some more. I nudged Sam's leg and pointed at the TV, but he ignored me.

It was happening again.

Last year, in fifth grade, we learned about these things called whirlpools. They were kind of like tornados, only in water, and they sucked things in if you got too close. Megan was Sam's whirlpool.

BE AWESOME

On Tuesday, my social studies teacher asked me to take something to the office for her a few minutes before the end of the period.

As I passed the library, someone called my name. I made sure I had my hall pass in case it was a teacher, but it wasn't. It was Madison, from my summer taekwondo class, and one of her friends.

I walked over. "Hey!"

"Hi!" Madison said.

"What happened?" I motioned to the crutches under her arms.

She looked sheepish. "Twisted my knee at cheerleading practice."

"That stinks," I told her.

I knew trying out for cheerleading wasn't Madison's idea. Madison was great at taekwondo, but her mom complained it wasn't a good sport for girls. She tested for her green belt the same day I tested for my yellow belt.

"Yeah, it does stink," Madison agreed. "But at least I get to sneak out of classes early." She nodded at Olivia, who was standing next to her and carrying a stack of books. "And I have a helper."

Olivia smiled but I could tell it was an I'm-just-being-polite one. (Rules to Surviving Sixth Grade No. 11: The table in the middle of the cafeteria belongs to the cheerleaders.)

Olivia sighed and shifted her hip, but Madison didn't budge. "How's taekwondo going?" Madison asked. "You're still going, right?"

I told her yep.

"Me too," she said. "The *dojang* is really cool. You should check it out." Because she was in the intermediate class, she went to Master Kim's actual training hall, instead of the community center like me.

"I go once a week, when I'm at my dad's. Well, at least I *did*." She looked down at her leg. "It may take me longer, but I'll get my next belt eventually."

I smiled. Madison wasn't a quitter, either.

"Anything else new?" she asked.

"I'm trying out for the play this afternoon," I told her.

"That's cool. Keep me posted."

"We better go," Olivia said. "The bell is going to ring soon."

She and Madison headed down the hall, but before they got too far, Madison turned around and called back to me. She told me the same thing she did right before my yellow-belt test.

"Remember. Don't be nervous, be awesome!"

TAP, TAP, TAP

Annie and I looked around the cafeteria. "I can't believe there are this many people auditioning," she said.

"Is that a good thing or a bad thing?" I asked her.

"Oh, it's good," she explained. "It means the show will be better because there are more actors to choose from."

"Yeah, but doesn't it also make it harder to get roles?"

"Well, for everyone else, sure," Annie said, and grinned. "But we're going to be aaawe-some."

Annie had been reading a book about plays and acting. At lunch, she highlighted entire pages.

"Okay," she said, pulling me aside. "Let's prepare."

Annie had planned out a pre-performance ritual for us. (Her book said every serious artist had one.) I felt silly doing it but it was what a BBF would do.

Annie stood in front of me and we whispered the rhyme she'd come up with.

Smile on,
shoulders back.
Hands on thighs,
tap, tap, tap.

Deep breath in,
spine straight.
Blink, blink, blink.
You'll do great!

"Let's break some legs!" Annie said when we were done. The day before, she told me it was bad luck to wish actors good luck. "In the theater, we say 'Break a leg,'" she said. I wondered how saying that would go over at a taekwondo test. Maybe "Break a board" would be more appropriate there.

Annie waved her hand to get my attention. "Hey? Ready? They're starting." I looked her in the eye so she knew I'd heard her. My medicine was starting to wear off. Sometimes I took a quick-release dose at home, but I wouldn't be able to do that here. The nurse had to be the one to give me a pill, and she left right after the last bell.

Annie and I walked over to the stage area. Mrs. Delany, the theater director, was standing there with a neon-pink plastic clipboard. She passed out name tags and we shared markers to fill them out.

"Here you go, Nimbus," some girl said, holding a marker in my direction. My stomach clenched but I didn't say anything. Annie made it super obvious she was examining the girl's name tag.

"Um. Why are you staring at my shirt?" the girl asked.

Annie shrugged. "Just memorizing your name for future reference," she said. The girl hurried off and I cracked up.

"Thanks," I told Annie. She said not to worry about it.

I recognized only a few of the kids who were auditioning. There were way more girls than boys, and everyone looked about as nervous as I felt. Which was a solid eight on a scale of one to ten. Okay, maybe a nine. I reminded myself that I was doing this for Annie. She needed me. And that's what best friends did—helped each other.

"Good afternoon, friends," Mrs. Delany called out. Annie and I shared a look. "Friends" is what our teachers back in elementary school called us. Most of the middle-school teachers said "folks" or "ladies and gentlemen" when they wanted our attention.

"Thank you all so much for coming today. Auditions are my favorite thing and we're going to have an absolute blast! I just know the fall show will be the best school production ever! The play we're doing is a humorous take on a classic. We're calling it *Cinder Ellen*. If you haven't heard of it before, that's because it was written by yours truly." Here, Mrs. Delany placed her hand on her chest and beamed. "This afternoon, what I'd like to do is get to know you all as performers. And to let you get to know each other as well. We'll begin with some improv."

THE QUICK VERSION OF WHAT MRS. DELANY TOLD EVERYONE ABOUT IMPROV

Improv" was short for "improvisation." It meant making things up on the spot. (And it was also Mrs. Delany's favorite thing.) It had four rules, so of course I liked it immediately because four was my favorite number. The rules were:

1. Don't overthink things.
2. Always say "Yes . . . and," which, as it turns out, doesn't mean to actually say the words. It means play along with whatever another person says and then add something to the scene.
3. Make statements. That means don't be wishy-washy when you're deciding how to respond.
4. Don't worry about making mistakes, because there is no such thing in improv. ("There are only *opportunities*.")

"I LOVE YOU, BABY."

The first game we played was called Tags.

Mrs. Delany split us into groups of five and designated one person to be the director. We got tags on strings with a character name and description. I got *Larry, ice cream truck driver.*

I looked across the room at Annie, who was in another group. She was smiling and holding up her tag, but I couldn't read it. I hadn't planned on being in separate groups and it made me more nervous.

The director of my group gave us a scene. We were supposed to be in a park on a summer Saturday afternoon. I yelled, *"Ice cream! Get your ice cream before it melts!"* in a deep voice and pretended to sell cones to the other characters. Then the director stopped us mid-scene and switched everyone's tags. I became *Daisy, playful puppy.*

That was more fun. All I did was pretend I was Bear. I even got down on my hands and knees and wagged my backside. Everyone laughed, which felt like the time everyone clapped for me at my yellow-belt test.

This kid named JJ got stuck with a tag that said *Frank, garbage man.* I thought that one would be hard, but JJ spent the whole time driving a pretend truck and asking, *"Pardonnez-moi,* have you any litter you'd like to lighten yourself of this fine afternoon?" When he came to me, he patted me on the head and said, "Good doggie."

After a while, Mrs. Delany called everyone over. "Now that we're all warmed up," she announced, "we're going to try my favorite improv staple, which will test your ability to stay in character. It's called 'I love you, baby.'"

When everyone stopped giggling, we broke up into two groups of twenty and made giant circles. I made sure Annie and I were together.

The game was simple, Mrs. Delany explained. One person stood in the middle of the circle and walked up to each person in the group. They had to say "I love you, baby. Won't you please give me a smile?" And the other person was supposed to say "I'm sorry, baby. But I just can't smile" without cracking up or breaking into any kind of smile. If they did, they had to sit down.

The tricky part was that the person could say the "I love you, baby" line any way they wanted. They could whisper or sing. They could be super serious or use a funny voice. They could do anything they wanted to. Stand on their head, act like a monkey, whatever. They just couldn't touch the person they were trying to get to smile.

An eighth grader named Paige went first. "I already know how to play, so I'll show you how it's done," she told everyone.

The girl next to Annie leaned over and whispered, "Paige is the all-time champion of this game. And she's a real, live professional. She was in a commercial when she was little."

Annie tried to act like that wasn't a big deal, but I

could tell she thought it was. "She lives behind me!" Annie told us.

Paige went around the circle. She got four people out right away just by saying "I love you, baby. Won't you please give me a smile?" in her regular voice.

After that, all it took was for her to say her line with any special voice. Once, she even yelled it. The boy was so surprised, he laughed even before she finished her line.

One by one, Paige got everyone to crack. Even Annie. (Who broke when Paige started to hop on one foot.)

Then she stepped in front of me.

"I JUST CAN'T SMILE."

Paige got right up in my face. "I love you, baby. Won't you please give me a smile?"

"I'm sorry, baby. But I just can't smile," I told her.

She tried again. This time, she said her line like a three-year-old. "I wuv you, babee. Peas give me a shmile?"

I kept my face as still as I could. "I'm sorry, baby. But I just can't smile."

Paige got even more creative. She tried singing the line, fake-crying it, standing behind me. She even did a hand-stand and said the line.

I didn't crack.

"Excellent work!" Mrs. Delany said. "What's your name?" she asked me.

"Eliza Bing," I told her.

Mrs. Delany told Paige to move on to the next person. I stayed standing.

We ran out of time before Paige could get to everyone else in the circle. The person from the other group had gotten out about half of his opponents.

"Okay, friends!" Mrs. Delany called out. "You did a wonderful job today. I hope you had fun. I hope I see each and every one of you back here tomorrow when we begin reading for parts."

Hold it right there, chocolate éclair!

I grabbed Annie's arm. "We have to come back tomorrow?" I asked. "You didn't tell me it was a two-day thing."

"Of course I did," Annie said. "So, how did you—"

"No, you didn't."

Annie nodded her head. "Yeah. I *did*. You probably forgot." I ignored the pang of sadness inside my chest. Annie usually didn't point it out when I forgot things.

"But there's no one to pick me up tomorrow," I told her. "My mom doesn't get off till five-thirty and my dad's got a late class. I'm supposed to take the bus and get off at my neighbor's house."

"Mo-mo can drop you off."

I was stuck like a baker fresh out of flour. I had only agreed to come to the first day of auditions so Annie wouldn't be alone. What if I bailed on her now and she dropped me like a burnt cookie? Operation BBF would be a bust after only a few days.

Nope. I couldn't let that happen.

"I can ask if that's okay," I said.

"*Yay!*" Annie squealed. "Thank you, thank you! You're the best."

What was it the school secretary had said when I remembered I had gym clothes I could wear? Oh yeah. *Crisis averted.*

Annie grinned. "You were sooo good at the smile game. How did you keep a straight face the whole time?"

I shrugged.

"No. For real. What's your secret?"

I wanted to tell her. (Best friends didn't keep secrets.) But I was embarrassed to tell her.

"I don't know. Beginner's luck?" I said.

WHAT I DIDN'T TELL ANNIE ABOUT KEEPING A STRAIGHT FACE DURING THE "I LOVE YOU, BABY" GAME

Here's the secret about not smiling: all I had to do was think of something else. Which was easy since my medicine had started to wear off.

While Paige was saying her line, I counted to ten in Korean in my head, tried to remember Sweet Caroline's recipe for fondant, and made a "Note to Self" to take my algebra book home. And when it got really hard, I just tried to figure out why no one had bothered to fix the clock on the wall that'd been stuck at 9:17 since the first day of school.

THE PART WHERE I TRIED TO CONVINCE MY PARENTS I'M NOT A BABY

At dinner, Dad asked how the auditions went.

"Pretty good," I said.

"Did you have fun?" Mom always asked me and Sam that. *Did you have fun at the marching competition? Did you have fun at taekwondo? Did you have fun doing the project?* I think it was her way of saying winning wasn't everything.

"Yeah, it was better than I thought it'd be," I told her. "But the auditions go for another day. Would it be okay if Annie's mom gives me a ride tomorrow?"

Mom frowned. "I suppose so. Do you know when you'll be back so I can let Mrs. Parker know when to expect you?" (Mrs. Parker was the neighbor who sometimes watched me.)

"Probably around the same time it was this afternoon."

"I guess that would be fine," Mom said. "I'm sure Mrs. Parker wouldn't mind, especially since it means you'd only be there for twenty minutes."

"Oooo, burn! People can only take twenty minutes of

you," Sam said on his way out the door for a late percussion practice.

"That's not what I meant and you know it," Mom called after him.

She turned to me. "That's not what I meant," she repeated.

I had an idea.

"Twenty minutes seems like an inconvenience for Mrs. Parker," I said carefully. "What if Annie's mom drops me at home and I hang out by myself until Dad gets here?"

Mom raised an eyebrow in Dad's direction. He gave her his I'm-staying-outta-this look.

Mom turned back to me. "Eliza, I'm not sure that's a good idea."

"Why not?" I asked. "Everyone else in my grade gets to stay home alone."

The last time I asked to stay home by myself was over the summer. Sam had to go to the community center and Dad had to take him because Mom had to work, and I didn't feel like getting dragged along.

Mom laughed and tried to be funny by saying, "Hello, go look in the mirror and introduce yourself to the girl there." I didn't think it was funny. Or fair. Plus, I was older and more mature now.

"But you've never done it," Mom argued. "And a lot could go wrong."

"In twenty minutes?" I asked.

"It only takes a few minutes for a house to burn down,"

Mom said. (Sometimes it stunk having a mom who was an ER nurse. They had loads of horror stories.)

"I'm not a baby anymore," I argued. "You should trust me."

"It's not that I don't trust you. . . ." Mom started.

"But how can I prove I can do it if you never let me try? You thought I'd quit taekwondo and I didn't. Doesn't that show I'm more responsible than I used to be?"

I could tell Mom was wavering.

"What's the worst that could happen?" I asked.

(Note to Self: Asking your mom "What's the worst that could happen?" is *not* a good idea.)

"I've already made plans with Mrs. Parker," Mom said, shaking her head. "Maybe another time."

Coconuts! I blew it.

HOW DAD SAVED THE DAY WITH ONE SENTENCE (OKAY, TECHNICALLY TWO)

She's right. The only way to see if she's ready is to give her a shot."

DAY TWO OF AUDITIONS, OR WHEN I LEARNED TO CHANNEL MY INNER NINJA PIG

On Wednesday, we read for parts. Mrs. Delany told us we'd be doing cold readings. According to Annie, "cold readings" meant you got up and read from the script without having a lot of time to prepare.

"The book says the secret is to focus on who your character is and their motivation," Annie told me. "And oh, don't death-grip the paper."

I wasn't sure what she meant about who my character was and what they wanted. But I understood death grip because that's what I did to my report when I had to stand up and read in front of my entire Spanish class.

Annie and I did our pre-performance ritual. *Tap tap tap. Blink blink blink.* Mrs. Delany handed out the pages we would be reading from. Everyone got the same double-sided pieces of paper with lines from various characters.

Mrs. Delany explained that her play combined *Cinderella* and a bunch of other fairy tales. Cinder Ellen was a cowgirl, and everyone was going to a barnyard bash instead of a ball. We'd be reading lines from Cinder Ellen, Deejay Razzy Ray, Humpty Grumpty, Jill, the Farmer, and Pig No. 1.

"When I call your name, please make your way to the stage," Mrs. Delany said. "I will let you know which character or characters to read for. Don't think or stress too much about it. Just do your best and have fun!"

Annie was excited when we found out we'd be going in alphabetical order. Her last name was Young-Mays. "You want to go at the end so you're the last person they remember," she whispered.

"Great," I whispered back. "I'll be one of the *first* people."

"Just make it memorable," Annie said.

Memorable? It was one thing when I made the people in my group laugh yesterday, but now I'd be in front of *everybody*! What if I did something like flooding-the-chem-lab memorable?

"Okay," Mrs. Delany called. "Here's the first group." She read a list of six names. It included Paige (her last name was Abraham) and me. Annie gave me a thumbs-up and I hurried onto the stage.

Paige stood onstage like she didn't mind one bit to go first. But I did.

Holy ta-moley! There were so many eyeballs on me. *Come on*, I told myself. *You can do this. A BBF joins in with her friend's activities.*

Mrs. Delany assigned parts and we started the scene.

Paige played Cinder Ellen. (She was great.) I read the part of Jill. Afterward, Mrs. Delany switched things up.

"Eliza, I'd like you to read for Pig No. 1," she said.

I'd stumbled over a few words when I'd read for Jill, so I was nervous about going again. I took a breath and remembered why I was there and what Annie said about focusing on who my character was.

But my character was a *pig*.

"Don't overthink it," Mrs. Delany told us. "Remember our improv rules and go!"

A boy named Jake started the scene off. My brain scrambled. I searched for a channel to land on. When I couldn't find one, I started reading my lines and hoped for the best.

Pig No. 1 didn't have that many lines. I mostly read them straight off the page. But near the end, something interesting happened. I started getting into it.

"*So,*" I read, pretending I was Sam and all teenager-y, "*I was telling my brother what he missed while he was taking his afternoon nap. And I said, 'The Notorious B.I.G. Wolf showed up and instead of blowing the door down, you know what he did?'*"—I paused here to build the suspense—"'*He kicked it!*'" Without thinking, I threw a push kick in the air to demonstrate and gave a sharp *kihap*. "*Huuup!*"

Out in the audience, I saw Annie clapping. A few other people were clapping, too. And Mrs. Delany was smiling!

Whoa.

~~TWENTY MINUTES~~
TEN MINUTES

"So, when will you find out if you got roles?" Annie's mom asked on the drive home.

"The cast list goes up at the end of the day Friday," Annie told her.

"Oooo. How exciting!" Mo-mo said.

Bingo, Annie's Chihuahua, crawled over us in the backseat. Mo-mo apologized. "It was raining all day, so he didn't get to go outside at doggie day care." I told her it was okay. Bingo always liked me. It was probably because he could smell Bear on my clothes.

Annie spent the whole ride talking about the auditions. Going with her had been a smart idea. It felt good to know what she was talking about.

Annie had read for Cinder Ellen and Humpty Grumpty. "I bet I talked too fast," she said. "I did. I talked too fast, didn't I?"

Annie always talked as fast as Bear could lick peanut butter off a spoon, so I didn't know what difference it would make to point that out. "No. You did great," I told her.

She grinned. "Thanks. You, too! And I think it's cool you took my advice about doing something memorable."

I tried to tell her the whole taekwondo kick just came out; it wasn't anything I planned. But she wasn't listening.

She kept saying how I'd made a "brave choice" and that her book said acting was all about making brave choices.

Annie may have thought I was brave, but I was definitely not feeling that way the closer we got to my house. I'd never been alone in the house before. Unless you counted that time Sam was at a friend's and Mom ran next door to borrow something from a neighbor and the smoke detectors went off. I was three. And taking a nap. So it wasn't my fault. Turns out it was dust in the system, but the fire trucks came anyway. Mom freaked out.

Annie and her mom watched me get the mail and then waited until I was safely inside the front door before waving and pulling away.

The house was quiet. I stood in the middle of the front hallway for a second and let my ears adjust. Who knew silence could be so loud?

Suddenly, Bear noticed someone was home and came running and barking around the corner.

"Hiya, girl," I said, leaning over to rub her curly poodle fur. "Did you miss me?" Bear licked me to tell me she did and then followed me into the kitchen.

"I guess it's just you and me"—I checked the oven clock—"for the next eighteen minutes. What kind of shenanigans shall we get into?"

Bear cocked her head. "How about a snack?" I suggested. I went to the fridge and grabbed a cold hot dog and gave her half. I chewed my half extra carefully since Mom always nagged me about eating too quickly. It wouldn't look good if I choked to death the first time I got to stay home alone.

After our snack, Bear pawed at the back door to be let out. "Hurry up," I told her. "I'm supposed to keep the doors locked at all times."

Bear came running back in a few minutes later. After she settled on the couch, I decided to start my homework. But I kept getting distracted, thinking about the auditions. It felt really good when people clapped and gave me high fives. I wondered if I had a shot at a speaking role. I bet Annie did.

Hummmmm.

What was that? The garage door was going up! No one was supposed to be home yet. *Maybe I should hide. Or call 911. Maybe I should do both.*

"Yo, E! I'm home!" It was Sam.

"What are you doing here?" I asked him.

"I live here, you dork."

"No. I mean, I thought you had marching band and then drum practice," I said.

He shrugged. "Mom asked if I could come home a little early to make sure you didn't destroy the house or get yourself kidnapped."

I scowled. Mom didn't even think I could manage on my own for twenty lousy minutes?

"I know how to escape from a kidnapper," I told him.

"Oh, right. You're a great and powerful yellow belt now."

"Why did you come through the garage?" I asked.

"You have my key. Speaking of which, give it back."

Sam never used to tease me. Not in a super mean way at least. But it felt different ever since he started dating—

A girl walked in from the garage. "Hi," she said. "I'm Megan."

FIRST IMPRESSION (SPOILER ALERT: BLAH)

Here's what I learned: doing your homework at the kitchen table is impossible when your big brother and his girlfriend are laughing and carrying on as if making nachos is the funniest thing in the world.

I grabbed my things so I could finish my work in my bedroom. But then Megan sat down, smiled, and shoved a bowl of nachos across the table.

"I wasn't sure how much cheese you like, so I didn't put much on," she said.

"Thanks," I said, taking a hot, cheesy chip. It was the polite thing to do, after all.

"So how do you like middle school?" Megan asked.

"It's okay."

"Do you play an instrument, too?"

I shook my head.

"I'm in the marching band," Megan said.

I know, I wanted to say. I knew a lot of things already because Sam wouldn't shut up. Megan was a sophomore like he was. She had a little brother. She wanted to be a preschool teacher. She took honors classes. Blah blah blah.

"I play clarinet," Megan told me.

I already knew that, too. I thought clarinets were cool. Maybe not as cool as drums, but when I did a report on Sweet Caroline for school, I found out she played clarinet. I didn't tell Megan that.

"We'll be in the living room," Sam told me. Megan followed him out.

Good. I could go back to my homework.

A little while later, though, they came back. Mom had texted Sam and said she was running late, and Megan thought it would be a nice surprise if she and Sam started dinner. We were having spaghetti, so it wasn't that hard.

Megan said I could work on the garlic bread if I wanted. I thought about it; I knew Mom would appreciate the help. But what I wanted was to be *anywhere* but there.

RULES TO SURVIVING SIXTH GRADE NO. 22: DON'T GET SO DISTRACTED WAITING FOR A LIST TO GO UP THAT YOU FORGET TO FOCUS ON A BIOLOGY QUIZ

THE PART WHEN THE CAST LIST GOES UP

Hurry up." Annie tapped her foot.

"I'm coming," I said. "I have to get my stuff first."

The two of us maneuvered our way through the halls toward the music room, where the cast list for *Cinder Ellen* was supposed to be. It seemed kinda mean of Mrs. Delany to make everyone wait until the end of the day. Especially since a lot of us had buses to catch. (Annie said her mom could give me another ride if I missed mine.)

We were just about to pass the woodshop room when a girl stepped in front of us.

"Hey! You're Nimbus," the girl said. "I heard about you!"

The old, familiar shame crawled up my cheeks. But Annie put her hand on her hip. "Her name is Eliza."

The girl studied us. I pretended I was playing the "I love you, baby" game and kept my face neutral. After a few seconds, she shrugged. "All right, whatever," she said, and walked away.

"Thanks," I mumbled.

"No problem," Annie said. "Now shake it off. We've got a list to look at!"

Annie and I made our way to the music room. The closer we got, the more nervous I became. What if Annie got a part and I didn't? I guessed I could sign up for the tech crew, but it wouldn't be the same. Annie said the tech crew didn't even start coming to rehearsals until the last few weeks. How could I be the best best friend ever if I didn't get to be with Annie?

There was a smallish crowd around the list, so we waited our turn. Annie grabbed my hand and we inched forward. At the very top of the page was:

Cinder Ellen . . . . . . Paige Abraham.

No big surprise there. Paige was a professional, after

all. She'd been on TV. I could've been on TV once. Over the summer, they filmed a *Sweet Caroline Cakes* episode at the community center's cake-decorating class. The class my parents wouldn't let me take.

Annie found her name in the middle of the list. "I'm the Nosy Neighbor!" She let go of my hand and hugged me.

"Yay!" I said.

Annie stopped hugging me, grabbed my hand again, and we checked the list.

"Look! Under 'Ensemble,'" she said. "You're Little Pig No. 3."

Wait. What?

"I got a part?" I asked. "For real?"

Annie pointed at the list again. "It's right there in black and white. See? I *knew* we'd both get parts. I knew it! Oh man, this is awesome. It's fate!"

I thought "fate" was a bit dramatic. But who cared? I got a part, and now Operation BBF was still on!

Annie and I moved out of the way so other people could check the list. At the very bottom, Mrs. Delany had written the date of the first rehearsal. There was also a note from her thanking everyone for auditioning and letting people know that if they didn't get a part, she hoped they'd please consider signing up for crew.

Annie and I practically ran to the parking lot and said goodbye. Thankfully my bus wasn't done loading, so I jumped in the line.

A pack of eighth graders walked by. (Rules to Surviving

Sixth Grade No. 17: Don't talk to eighth graders unless they talk to you first.)

"Hey, Paige!" I called. She stopped and looked around. "Congratulations on getting the lead," I told her. I was breaking the rule, but I didn't care. I was excited about the cast list.

Her friends pretended not to hear me. But Paige looked right at me.

"Thanks, Eliza," she said. Then she swung her ponytail and led the pack away.

Paige knew my name. That was a good thing, right?

DO MONKEYS HAVE TAILS?

Mom came home from work with a store-bought cake.

"Well," she asked, "is this a congratulatory cake or a consolatory cake?"

I wasn't sure what the second kind of cake was, but since I'd made the cast list I knew it was the first.

My family cheered when I told them. Well, okay, Sam just gave me a fist bump and said, "Cool."

Mom had frosting in a tube, too. I wanted to decorate the cake (I was the expert, after all), but she insisted on piping out "Congrats!" herself.

"It's not every day that your daughter lands a role in the school play," she said.

"It's a small role," I told her. "I probably don't even have any lines."

"There are no small roles," Mom declared. "Only small actors!" I rolled my eyes at her.

Mom asked when the play was and I told her I didn't know yet. "Well, just let me know as soon as possible so I can ask for the night off."

Mom hardly ever took time off. In fact, the last time I remember her doing that was when I fell down the stairs and went to her ER. That was fun. Not the ER or the getting-X-rays-of-my-butt part. But Mom, Dad, and I had a pizza party while we waited in the exam room. And when we got home, Mom sat on the couch next to me until I went to bed.

"Will you come to the play?" I asked Sam.

He shrugged. "Sure thing, E. I bet Megan would go, too." A tiny sigh escaped before I could catch it.

"So what about me?" Dad teased. "Don't you care if your favorite dad shows up? I'm hurt."

I laughed. "Okay. What about you?" I asked him. "Are you going to come, too?"

"Do monkeys have tails?" Dad asked. It was an old family joke. (FYI, the answer is yes.)

RE-BREAKABLE

During taekwondo on Monday, I noticed that my nail polish was chipped on my left big toe. I tried to push it out of my brain. Master Kim was watching. Plus, I needed to be concentrating on counting jumping jacks. Everyone was taking turns and I was next.

"*Hana, dool, set, net, dasut,*" the yellow belt to the right of me counted. He kept going until he got to ten. "*Yasut, ilgop, yuldol, ahop, yul!*"

Counting to twenty was part of my gold-belt test requirements. It wasn't too hard since all you had to remember was to add *yul,* or "ten," in front of all the numbers.

"*Yul hana, yul dool, yul set,*" I called out, remembering to count slowly and loudly, "*yul net, yul dasut, yul yasut, yul ilgop, yul yuldol, yul ahop . . . seumul!*"

I had trouble remembering what twenty was at first. But then Dad pointed out that "*seumul*" sounded kinda like "Samuel." "So," he said, "just think to yourself, 'I don't need *twenty* brothers, I already have one. Samuel!'" Dad was really good at coming up with mnemonic devices. (Those are tricks to help you remember something.) Maybe I'd have him help me memorize my lines for the play. That is, 1) if I had any and 2) if he wasn't too busy.

"Class, make two lines," Master Kim called. I got in Miss Abigail's line. Miss Abigail was a teenage black belt. I saw her do a flying side kick over two people at a demonstration during the summer. It was so cool that it made me want to come back to class after I'd thought I was going to quit.

"We will be practicing our board breaks," Master Kim announced. Everyone got excited when he picked out two re-breakable boards. Those were plastic boards that had interlocking tabs down the middle so you could break them and put them back together. Master Kim handed Miss Abigail one.

I watched as everyone in front of me practiced. (As Master Kim says, "a good martial artist focuses their mind and body.") Each belt level had their own board break. When it was my turn, Miss Abigail asked what my break was so she could position the board. It was our responsibility to know our test requirements.

"I have hammer fist, ma'am," I said.

We normally practiced on kicking paddles or small, padded shields. I'd never practiced on a re-breakable board before. It was about the same size and thickness as a real board. I wondered what it would feel like to hit it.

I stepped back into a fighting stance and balled my right hand into a fist. All I had to do was to raise it up and then bring it down on the board like my hand was the head of a hammer. I *kihaped*. "*Huuup!*"

Owwww!

The edge of my hand stung like crazy. I pulled it back immediately and inspected my pinky.

"You okay?" Miss Abigail asked. I shook my hand to show her it hurt, but she just held the board up again.

"Give it another try," she said.

I made a fist, pulled it back, and tried again. But my hand just smacked the board and bounced off. I rubbed the side of my hand.

"You're not following through," Miss Abigail said. "Aim past the board."

But that wasn't the problem. That was something I learned over the summer. You had to imagine aiming your kick or punch *past* something, not *at* it. The problem was that I had to take my first test in the summer with an injury. I didn't want to break myself again.

"It'll hurt," I told Miss Abigail.

She gave me a sympathetic smile. "Remember, what you feed, grows."

"Huh?"

"It's an expression," she said. "It means you're paying attention to your fear. Pay attention to your technique instead."

I tried one more time.

Smack! *Owww!*

"Don't worry," Miss Abigail said brightly. "We'll keep working on it."

That was easy for her to say. She had a black belt tied around her waist.

FIRST REHEARSAL

Everyone crowded around Mrs. Delany on the stage.

"First off, let me thank you all for being here and give you a big congratulations," she said. "I can't tell you how excited I am you're going to be a part of this fall's production. We only have nine weeks to prepare, but I'm confident because this is the most talented group I've ever had!"

Annie leaned in and whispered, "I bet she says that every year." I giggled. And so did a few other people who overheard her. But no one seemed to mind.

"Now, I've been a director long enough to know that none of you are going to listen to anything else I have to say until I pass out the scripts," Mrs. Delany continued. "So queue up, and let's do my favorite thing—the traditional Passing of the Scripts!"

Annie and I were in the middle of the line. It wasn't like at taekwondo, though. At taekwondo, everyone was quiet and waited patiently. Onstage, everyone talked and bounced and swayed like helium balloons on strings.

"Here you go, Eliza," Mrs. Delany said when she handed me my copy.

Holy honeybees! I loved how the script felt in my hand. It was a little bigger than a paperback book (only not nearly as thick) and had a pale blue cover. There was a drawing of a ball gown and a barn on it. Across the middle was *Cinder Ellen: A Fractured Fairy Tale of Barnyard Proportions.* And at the bottom: *Written by Tabitha Delany.* The best part? The spine creaked when I opened it. Getting to be the first person to open a book is like getting to be the first person to walk outside after it snows.

Mrs. Delany said she'd give everyone time to read the script and explore their parts. Annie and I parked ourselves in a corner, sitting back to back.

"This reminds me of sleepaway camp," Annie joked. "We used to sit this way when we ran out of camp chairs." I'd never been to sleepaway camp. Shoot. I'd never even had a sleepover. I wanted to invite Annie but I worried she wouldn't want to come.

The two of us took turns reading our character descriptions out loud. Annie was Nosy Neighbor. The description was *"cranky, gray-haired lady, calls the police about party noise."*

Annie sighed and turned around so we were facing each other.

"What?" I asked.

"I don't know. It's just that it sounds a little boring."

"Are you kidding?" I said. "You get to be a villain. That sounds like fun."

Annie smiled. "You're right."

"Plus," I added, "someone has to call. It's an important role."

I didn't know if this was actually true since we hadn't read the whole script yet. But it sounded believable and I wanted Annie to be as excited as I was. Best friends want each other to be happy.

"What does your description say?" Annie asked.

"Mine says *funny and talkative*," I read, "*the baby of the group*."

"That's you!" Annie said.

"Do we have any lines?" I wondered.

"Let's see!"

Annie and I raced through the pages. "Found one!" Annie exclaimed a few minutes later. We high-fived. "And here's three more!"

"I've got three," I told her.

"How many words altogether?" Annie asked.

I counted. "Twelve."

"Twelve? For three lines?"

"Well, one of the lines is just me saying 'Gesundheit' after someone sneezes."

"I've got twenty-nine words."

I wasn't sure why Annie cared about how many lines or words we got to say. Maybe there was something in her theater book I should know about. I decided to ask Mom and Dad if I could get my own copy.

MRS. DELANY'S RULES FOR SCRIPTS

1) Write your name in it.
2) Treat it with care: no eating around it or tossing it around. ("Water is okay as long as it's in a water bottle.")
3) Always bring it to rehearsal.
4) Always bring it to rehearsal.
5) Always bring it to rehearsal.

SCHEDULING CONFLICTS

After dinner, I pulled out the form we got at the end of rehearsal.

"We're supposed to write down scheduling conflicts we have so Mrs. Delany can plan accordingly," I told Mom.

Mom grabbed the family calendar off the wall. The first thing she did was mark opening night and draw a big star around it. "Football season will be over by then, so we don't have to worry about a game. But we won't be able to go to the Saturday matinee. Sam and I have the Battle of the Marching Bands competition that day." Mom went to all the marching-band events to tape up twisted ankles or help if someone passed out.

"So. Looks like you have rehearsals on Tuesdays, Thursdays, and Fridays," Mom continued. "That works out great since taekwondo is on Mondays and Wednesdays. For once, the stars are aligned in our favor." Mom made a note in each box and then highlighted them. Everyone had their own color highlighter. Mine was pink. Sam's was blue. Mom's was yellow. And Dad's was green. It made our calendar look like a weird rainbow puzzle.

"It'll be a challenge, but that *should* work out," she said, more to herself than to me. "I might have to ask Annie's mom if you can carpool with them, though. And we'll have to pay Mrs. Parker." (At least she didn't add "to babysit." I wasn't a baby.)

Mom turned to Dad. "Honey, do you think you'll be able to leave right after class on Tuesdays so you can beat the traffic?"

Dad frowned. "I can't. My new seminar starts next week and it's on Tuesdays."

Mom stopped highlighting and looked up. "What do you mean?"

"My new seminar at school," Dad said. But Mom only stared.

"You know? The one I told you about," Dad said.

"You most certainly did not," Mom said.

I squirmed in my seat. Being in the play seemed to complicate things.

"Yes. I did," Dad said evenly. "I won't be able to get home on Tuesdays until five-thirty. At the earliest."

"But who's going to be here for Eliza?" Mom asked. "My shift doesn't end until five and Sam has band practice. We can't keep imposing on poor Mrs. Parker."

No one said anything for a good thirty seconds. They didn't expect me to quit the play, did they?

"Um. I could stay home alone," I offered. "It went okay last time."

Mom chewed her lower lip.

"I didn't burn down the house or get kidnapped or anything," I said.

Dad laughed. "It's true. There wasn't any bloodshed."

Mom was still stone-faced.

"It's only for a couple of hours," I said. "I can do it." And I really meant it.

Finally, she gave in. "I guess we don't have much choice."

I wished she sounded more confident. But it was a start. And I'd just have to prove she could trust me.

OW WOW WOW

Heads up, you have to warm up in theater just like you do at taekwondo class.

"Okay, friends," Mrs. Delany called. "Our bodies are our instruments, so let's wake up those muscles and tune those voice boxes!"

Annie and I found spots near each other and gave ourselves room like Mrs. Delany instructed.

"Let's shake!" Mrs. Delany called. "Noggins first!" Then she demonstrated by moving her head side to side and all around.

I looked around. The kids who'd been in plays before started moving right away. They didn't seem to care how silly they looked. Annie caught my eye and then shrugged. The two of us began nodding our heads, too. A little at first, then more.

It wasn't like when I got caught in the safety shower. No one was paying attention to me. Everyone was busy doing their own thing.

"Now shake those arms!" Mrs. Delany called. "Get those hands moving, too!" We all stopped shaking our heads and began flailing our arms instead.

For the next minute or so, Mrs. Delany called out body parts and we shook them.

"Arms!"

"Legs!"

"Try your torso!"

"Now just your elbows!"

Then suddenly Mrs. Delany yelled, *"Earthquake!"*

The veteran theater kids were all shaking everything at once and staggering around like the ground was moving. A kid nearby bumped into Annie, who then bumped into me. The two of us joined the "earthquake" and laughed along with everyone else.

After Mrs. Delany got us settled, she had us stand up straight and put our hands on our belly buttons. When we breathed in, we were supposed to use our lungs to push on our hands to make sure we were using our full lung capacity.

"Everybody say 'Ow,'" Mrs. Delany called.

"Ow."

"Everybody say 'Wow,'" she said.

"Wow."

"One more!"

"Wow."

"Put it all together now."

"Ow wow wow!"

We did a few more sound chants. (*Pah-teak-ca! Bah-teak-ca!*) As long as Annie and I didn't look at each other, I could do it without cracking up.

Mrs. Delany declared we were sufficiently warm, and we all sat down in a semicircle on the stage. There were twenty-six people in the cast. (Annie said it was lucky to have an even number, and since my favorite number [four] was even, I thought so, too.)

"Today, we'll be doing one of my favorite things," Mrs. Delany said. "A read-through!"

I quickly figured out this meant we'd be reading the play out loud together.

"Now, this is supposed to be fun," Mrs. Delany told us. "I don't expect perfection. We're all getting to know each other."

The play opened with Cinder Ellen (Paige) and her stepmother (played by a girl named Kayla) fighting about Cinder Ellen cleaning out the barn. Cinder Ellen's stepbrother and stepsister joined in. It was a funny scene, and Paige had most of her lines from the first two pages memorized.

Best friends have private conversations, so I nudged Annie and nodded in Paige's direction. "Show-off," I whispered.

Annie frowned. "Paige is just being professional." Her words smarted like a bee sting.

"Sorry to interrupt, friends," Mrs. Delany said. "I just wanted to make sure everyone understands that I don't expect anyone to have their lines memorized yet." She paused and looked around the group, smiling. "I won't ask you to be off-book for at least a few weeks. Please continue."

I guessed "off-book" meant not relying on your script to say your lines. Speaking of the script, Paige looked down at hers when Mrs. Delany was talking. It looked like her cheeks were pink, but I couldn't tell from across the stage.

As it got closer and closer for me to say my first line, my

hearted pounded as fast as Bear's after she runs down the stairs. But in a good way.

Mr. Goat (played by a kid named Anthony) faked a sneeze.

"Gesundheit!" I said.

Then right after I said it, Anthony sneezed for real. "I said *gesundheit!*" I didn't plan to do that. My mouth forgot to consult my brain ahead of time.

But everyone laughed. And I felt as light as fluffy white frosting.

TICK TOCK

At the next rehearsal, Mrs. Delany had us break into groups. I sat with the rest of the people who were in the party scene. Annie sat on the other side of the stage with the cast members in her scene.

"One of the most important aspects of storytelling is character development," Mrs. Delany announced. "Before you can step into the soul of your character, you must know who they are."

Master Kim said something like that once. Only it was about walking around in someone else's shoes, even though we went barefoot in class.

Mrs. Delany continued, "You need to know your

character's backstory. It will tell you *how* they fit into the story, and *why* they are onstage."

Vivian (Little Pig No. 2) spoke up. "But if you wrote the play, don't you already know?"

Mrs. Delany smiled. "Yes. But it's not important for me to know, it's important for *you* to know."

This sounded a little hokey. Like when Dad told me I should decide on my own punishment for forgetting to turn off the faucet and overflowing the sink. (FYI, I didn't forget. I wanted to see if the little hole at the top of the basin worked.)

"Today," Mrs. Delany said, "I want you to explore your character's backstory. Who is your character? What makes them go tick tock?"

Paige rolled her eyes when Mrs. Delany said this last part. I didn't see what the big deal was. Mrs. Delany had funny ways of saying things sometimes. So what?

Everyone got out their scripts (*Rules 3 through 5: Always bring it to rehearsal*), and Mrs. Delany passed out paper since we had to leave our backpacks on the floor in front of the stage. Along with our scripts, we were supposed to bring a pencil to every rehearsal.

"Shoot," I whispered.

JJ (Little Pig No. 1) whispered back. "What?"

"My pencil isn't sharp."

"So what?" Vivian said. "It'll still write, right?"

"I hate dull pencils. I need a sharp one," I said, trying not to panic.

JJ motioned to the back of the stage. "I think there's one of those sharpeners you crank on the wall."

I crept backstage and found it. By the time I returned, Mrs. Delany was already giving instructions.

"I want you to take some time and really think about this," Mrs. Delany said. "For example, if your character doesn't have a name, give them one. If they already have a first name, give them a last one. Write down your character's age and where they live. Tell me about their family. Do they have any siblings or pets? What's their happiest memory? Tell me about their most embarrassing moment or a secret they have. Read through your script and see if it gives you any clues. Get creative. And remember, there are no wrong answers."

I got busy with the exercise. Right away, I decided my character's name was Julia and she had a goldfish named Sprocket. I didn't know her last name yet. "Pig" seemed boring.

There were twelve of us playing party guests, and we all helped each other.

"What do chickens even eat?" Miles asked.

Kate looked it up on her phone. "Greens, such as weeds, grass, and vegetables, and they also peck the dirt for bugs. Or just chicken feed from the pet store."

"What hobby should my character have?" Paul wondered.

"What kinds of things do you like to do?" I asked him.

"How old should I make my character?" Vivian said.

"Forty-two," JJ answered. "The answer to any question you don't know is forty-two."

"I'm not making my character forty-two," Vivian complained. "She can be sixteen."

Mrs. Delany walked around and checked in with everyone. When she got to me, she pointed to my note about Sprocket and said, "That's my favorite!"

WHAT I READ WHEN IT WAS MY TURN TO SHARE

Character: Little Pig No. 3
Name: Julia (no last name)
Age: fourteen
Siblings: one brother (Little Pig No. 1) and one sister (Little Pig No. 2)
Pet: goldfish named Sprocket
Favorite subject in school: mud mixing
Least favorite subject: barn building
Wants to be: marine biologist
Favorite thing about self: curly tail
Hobbies: kicking doors open and making cakes
Happiest memory: going on a tractor ride with Farmer Ted

Most embarrassing moment: once sneezed really loud in the middle of the library

Secret: allergic to corn

Three words that describe her personality: funny, talkative, kind

WHAT PAIGE SAID

Nicely done," Mrs. Delany told me. "Does anyone have any feedback for Eliza?"

Several hands went up.

"Yes, Paige?" Mrs. Delany prompted. I straightened my back. Paige Abraham had advice for *me*?

"I liked the part about the mud mixing class," Paige said sweetly. "But maybe you could have made your character's embarrassing moment taking a shower at school."

Paige held my gaze while people snickered. I looked away first.

"I'm not sure I understand," Mrs. Delany said.

"Oh, I was just brainstorming," Paige told Mrs. Delany. "You know. How people have dreams about arriving late for a test or forgetting to wear clothes."

Mrs. Delany ignored the giggles and called on two more people to share their feedback. I pretended to listen to them.

After rehearsal, JJ came over to me. "Paige is a jerk," he said.

"Yeah," Vivian agreed.

I looked around for Annie. Annie always knew how to make me feel better. But she was on the side of the stage, talking to Paige.

ONE BIG, HAPPY

I had no desire to be anywhere near them, but I was riding home with Annie. So I headed in their direction.

I imagined their conversation in my head:

What you said about Eliza's character was hilarious, Annie says.

I know, right? Paige responds. *It just came to me.*

My stomach sank as I moved closer.

"Of course this is my business," Annie was saying. "She's my friend."

Paige smirked when she noticed me. "Were your ears burning?" she asked.

Annie pulled on my elbow until I was standing next to her. "It wasn't nice," she told Paige. "You owe Eliza an apology."

Phew! Annie was on my side!

Paige rolled her eyes. "For what? Mrs. Delany asked us to give feedback, and I gave her feedback. I was *trying* to help. You're the one reading more into this."

Annie hesitated, as if she was considering Paige's

explanation. But I thought Paige knew exactly what she was doing. And she'd said it in front of everyone. The only way she could've been more obvious was if she'd called me Nimbus.

Paige went on. "Actors are supposed to draw on real-life experiences," she said. "Believe me or don't believe me. I really don't care. Either way, I'm outta here."

Annie and I watched her float out of the cafeteria. "Thanks for sticking up for me," I said after Paige was gone.

Annie turned to me and smiled. "I've always got your back."

I should've known that. People didn't call me Nimbus much anymore, but when they did, Annie confronted them or used her mind trick where she took out a pen and asked their name like she was going to report them. When she wasn't around, I ignored them.

Annie and I made our way toward the parking lot and climbed into Mo-mo's car. "Your character development was awesome, by the way," I told her.

"Thanks!" Annie said. "I really liked yours, too."

I cheered up even more when Annie's mom handed Bingo to me over the seat. "Here. He missed you."

If Annie and I ever had a sleepover, maybe she could bring Bingo. I bet he and Bear would get along as well as Annie and I did.

"Tell me about your character thingy," Annie's mom said. "I need details."

Annie and I laughed. Then Annie gave her mom the

rundown. She'd decided her character's name was Mrs. Riesczecks. Her mom cracked up. Apparently, that was a cranky neighbor of theirs with blue hair.

"Maybe we can get you a wig and spray-paint it blue," I suggested. Annie agreed this was an excellent idea.

"My book says looking the part can help you get into character," she said.

Annie rattled off the rest of her character's traits for her mom.

"My favorite part was her being a retired lunch lady!" I said.

"Yeah. Monica liked that part, too!"

"Monica?"

"You know," Annie insisted. "She plays the Dairy Godmother."

"Oh. Right."

"Hey!" Annie said excitedly. "I just thought of something to add in our Rules to Surviving guide. What about: 'Talk to at least one new person a day'?"

"Sure," I said.

While Annie pulled out the notebook and wrote it down, I thought about it more. I talked to JJ and Vivian. So Annie talking to other people was okay, too. Best friends were understanding. I wasn't worried. After all, Mrs. Delany said a cast was like one big, happy family.

AFTER REHEARSAL ON FRIDAY, OR WHEN I'M HOME ALONE MINUS THE SLED

I stared at the front door as if that would make it magically unlock.

Soggy pretzels! Dad said to remind him to give me the spare key and I forgot. And then he forgot. No one was due home for another hour, and I had accidentally left my phone on the kitchen counter this morning.

Now what? Mom would never let me stay home again if she came home and found me sitting on the front step. Or frozen to death. (Okay, fine. It wasn't *that* cold.)

I took a deep breath. We learned in taekwondo that remembering to breathe could help keep you from panicking in an emergency. Not that this was a full-blown emergency. More like a roadblock.

Wait. Road, car. Duh, I thought. *The garage.*

I walked over and punched in the code. I made sure the door was all the way down, too, before I went in the house. Mom would freak out if she came home and the door was open. She worried about someone walking in and stealing our bikes and tools.

I remembered how eerie the house was last time, so I called, "Bear! I'm home!" right away. She came running and barking.

Mom had left a note for me.

Rules:
Make sure the front door is locked.
Homework first.
If the phone rings, let the machine get it. (If it's me or Dad, we'll leave a message and you can call back.)
If someone comes to the door, don't answer it!
You can let Bear out but lock the door once she comes back in.
Don't go anywhere.

A little ways down, after the rest of the list, Mom added:

Have fun.

After I put my backpack away and kicked off my shoes, I made myself a bowl of ice cream with whipped cream and mini chocolate chips on top. I'd wanted to do that ever since I saw Kevin eat his humongous sundae in *Home Alone*. (FYI: *Home Alone* is a movie about a boy who accidentally gets left behind when his family goes on a trip at Christmastime. At first, Kevin goes a little crazy having fun, sledding down the stairs, and eating a bunch of junk food. And, oh, there are a couple of funny burglars who try to rob his house, so Kevin sets up booby traps.)

It was important Mom knew I could be trusted, so I made sure to clean up my mess. (Plus, I kinda didn't want her to know I'd eaten ice cream in the middle of the day.) Mom's note said *Homework first*, but having the house all to myself for an hour was too cool to waste on a chapter about the influence of geography on the development of ancient civilizations.

I flipped on the TV and tried to sit down on the couch to watch, but my arms and legs felt jittery, like someone had plugged them in. So after pressing OFF on the remote, I stood in the middle of the living room.

The first thing I did was spin until I was dizzy.

Then I did a few front kicks in the air. "*Huuup!*"

My voice echoed off the walls and wooden floor, sounding extra loud. "Echo," I said. Then louder: "*Echo!*"

Bear looked confused. "Don't worry," I told her, and laughed.

The doorbell rang.

My laugh got stuck in my throat. But Bear found her voice super quick.

Bark! Bark! Bark!

"Shhh," I told her.

Then the person knocked on the door. It wouldn't be Sam. He was still at band practice and even if he'd come home early, he'd probably use the garage door like he did before.

Whoever was at the door rang the bell and knocked again.

No one's home, I tried to say with my mind. *Go away.*

Knock, knock, knock. (Bark, bark, bark!)

I ninja-ed my way to the front door, trying to keep my heart from beating too loudly. When I got there, I stretched on my toes to look through the peephole. There was a man there, just off the front step. He was wearing a black jacket and had a messenger bag on his shoulder. He looked like some kind of a salesperson.

Should I just answer it?

Mom said not to, but what if the guy was there casing the place to rob? If he thought no one was home, he'd break in. Maybe I should flick the porch light on just to let him know someone was there. While I debated what to do, he knocked again. I jumped back a little, which made Bear bark even more.

If I'd been Kevin from *Home Alone*, I could've used a recorded clip from a video to scare the guy away. But I didn't have any booby traps. All I had was a yellow belt.

I took a deep breath and remembered what Miss Abigail said in taekwondo class about not feeding fear.

Standing perfectly still, I waited until the man gave up and left. Then I peeked out the window to make sure he'd really moved on.

When Dad came home an hour later, I was sitting at the kitchen table working on social studies.

"Hi, honey. How'd it go?" he asked.

"Piece of cake," I told him.

"BACK FALL!"

Miss Abigail helped Master Kim unroll a giant, square mat in the middle of the room.

"We are going to work on falls today," Master Kim told our class.

A couple of people said "Yes!" and pumped their fists. And everyone hurried to find a spot along the mat. Because we trained at the community center, we didn't get to practice falls very often. The carpet was the short, stiff kind that gives you rug burns. Thankfully, when I first started training, my feet were already toughened up because it was summer and I went barefoot a lot.

Each person took a turn being in the middle of the mat with Master Kim while everyone else watched. White belts went first.

"The most important thing with any fall," Master Kim said, "is to protect your head."

Master Kim showed a white belt how to crouch down and cross his arms.

"Tuck your head," Master Kim told the boy. "Drop your chin to your chest.

"Now, roll back slowly."

Master Kim put his hand on the boy's back and guided him as the boy teetered backward.

"Back fall!" Master Kim said. I'm not sure why, but

Master Kim always called out which fall you were supposed to be doing.

When the boy hit the ground, he smacked both of his hands flat beside him on the mat, and let out a *kihap* like he was supposed to.

"Good," Master Kim told the boy.

After the rest of the white belts practiced, the yellow belts were up.

Rolling backwards while you were low wasn't too hard. But yellow belts had to start their rolls from a standing position. It was a lot harder, and I was still getting used to it.

I stood in the middle of the mat and crossed my arms.

"Drop your chin to your chest," Master Kim reminded me. "And . . . back fall!"

My body wouldn't budge.

I giggled nervously.

"Trust your skills," Master Kim told me. But it wasn't me I didn't trust. It was gravity!

"Go slowly if you need to," Master Kim said. "Pretend you are sitting down in a chair."

I tried again and imagined myself sitting down. When I was about halfway down, Master Kim said, "Back fall!"

I rolled back in a half-sit-half-fall and smacked my hands on the mat like I was supposed to.

"Good," Master Kim told me. "Next time remember to *kihap*."

"Yes, sir," I said, and bowed before heading back to my spot.

Remembering to *kihap* was hard sometimes. Especially when your brain was busy thinking about what your body was supposed to be doing. Plus, it still felt weird to yell. Inside. With other people around.

Everyone had a different *kihap*. Mine sounded like *huuup* but I'd been trying out new ones. Like *hiiice* and *i-oisk*. (That's how Master Kim's spirit yell sounded.)

The thing was, the way a *kihap* sounded was something that happened without you thinking. It was automatic, like a sneeze. And the way you say "Gesundheit."

ONE BIG, CRASHING FAMILY

We'd just finished our vocal warm-up and were standing in an arc on the stage.

"The other day we worked on developing our characters," Mrs. Delany told the cast. "Today, I'd like to warm up with some physicality exercises."

"What's physic-reality?" I whispered to Annie.

"It's physic*ality*," Annie said. "It means . . ."

Mrs. Delany stopped talking and looked straight at Annie. Annie's face turned pink. Shoot. Getting your friend in trouble was definitely the opposite of being a BBF.

Mrs. Delany went on. "Physicality is a very important

thing for an actor to have in their tool kit," she said. "It refers to the way an actor moves, or uses his or her body to become the character from head to toe."

Physicality. Tool kits. I swear. Sometimes being in theater was like visiting a foreign country with a different language.

"So," Mrs. Delany explained, "if my character walked this way"—she strutted across the stage—"what would you know about her?"

We decided it meant she was confident or in charge.

"And if my character moved this way"—Mrs. Delany walked around slowly with her arms swinging back and forth in front of her—"what does that show you?"

Someone suggested that the character was big or maybe old. Someone else said it showed the character was lazy.

"Think about your character," Mrs. Delany said. "Now. I want you to *move* like your character."

A few people began to move, but most everyone stood still.

"Don't think," Mrs. Delany said. "Move. Try something. If it doesn't feel right, try something else."

Mom and Mrs. Delany would totally get along. Mom liked to say you should try a decision on for size like a coat. That way you can walk around in it for a bit and see how it feels. I did that over the summer, when I was trying to decide if I should quit taekwondo after getting in trouble with Master Kim for horsing around in class.

I glanced over at JJ and Vivian, the other Little Pigs.

They were both standing upright and kind of waddling around. I waddled, too. Only I stood on my tippy-toes because pigs have hooves, and I always thought that's what it looked like they were doing. Then I decided my character wouldn't waddle. She'd walk around a room like a model. But that didn't feel quite right, either. So then I had her walk with a slouch, like Sam did sometimes.

Everyone kept moving around and trying out different walks. Annie's character was an old lady, so she was hunched over and shuffling slowly. Other people started to get a little too into it and act wild. Pretty soon the stage was as chaotic as a chicken coop with a fox inside.

"Whoa! Watch it!" someone said.

"You ran into me!" was the reply.

"Do you mind?"

And it wasn't just the people playing the barnyard animals.

"Hey. I need more room. Go do that somewhere else!"

"Seriously. No one cares. You're just part of the background scenery."

"*Freeze!*" Mrs. Delany yelled. We all stopped. Mrs. Delany never yelled.

"Gather up. *NOW.*"

Whatever was coming was not going to be good.

BACK FALL!

We regrouped into our arc and sat down.

"Friends, there's been some discord and misinformation," Mrs. Delany began. "And that needs to end immediately."

We all looked at each other nervously.

"I overheard some very disrespectful comments just now. Let me be clear: there are no small roles," Mrs. Delany said. "Every single character has a purpose. If you think your role is more important than someone else's just because you may be onstage more often or have more lines, I'm here to tell you that you are wrong.

"While working on this production, we are a family and I expect you to act like one. Which means treating each other with respect. Make no mistake, the play is the priority and if I see someone is not being supportive or is getting a big ego, I will ask that person to leave the show. Does everyone understand?"

We nodded our heads.

Mrs. Delany clapped once and smiled. "Great! Moving forward, I think we need to see how much we rely on one another. Everybody up! Come on and make a circle. We're going to do my favorite bonding activity."

Once we'd made the circle, Mrs. Delany asked us to take a few steps toward the circle's center. "Get in nice and tight," she said. "I'm pretty sure everyone has bathed recently. We don't smell that bad."

We laughed.

"Everyone turn so their left shoulder is facing the inside of the circle. Now, take two steps sideways."

She waited until we were all facing the same direction, nice and tight. "Next. Place your hands—gently!—on the shoulders of the person in front of you."

More giggles. What were we going to do? Rub each other's backs or something? That would be weird. Sometimes in taekwondo we had to grab each other's shoulders, but that's because we were about to do an escape. Plus, at taekwondo everyone had on *doboks*, which were long-sleeved and made from a heavy material. JJ was in front of me and had a T-shirt on. He felt sweaty. *Ewww.*

"On the count of three," Mrs. Delany said, "I want everyone to slowly sit down, like you're easing into a chair."

Wait. What?

"One, two, three!"

Everyone giggled as we sat down on the lap of the person behind us. Which, of course, meant someone was also sitting on *your* lap! (Although that was only sorta true in my case; JJ was doing his best to squat and not actually sit on my lap.)

The giant lap-sitting thing shouldn't work but it did. We were holding each other up!

"Hold it!" Mrs. Delany called. "Hooold it! Nice job, friends. We can do it. Let's go for ten!"

Mrs. Delany and the cast began counting the seconds. And laughing. We got to eight before things started to fall apart. Too much wiggling and laughing meant people were sliding off laps and standing up.

I felt the girl whose lap I was sitting on shift. A few seconds later, I was falling. My brain went *Ahhhh! Now what?* Then something really weird happened. I heard Master Kim's voice in my head.

Back fall!

I tucked my chin and sat down in slow-mo. As I rolled back, I slapped my arms and hands on the ground beside me. Sweet baby oranges!

"Are you okay?" JJ asked. I nodded and he held out his hand to help me up. "Your fall was kinda cool."

"Thanks."

Huh. I guess that's why Master Kim always yelled at us mid-fall in class. It made your body remember what to do even if your brain didn't.

THE PART WHERE I GOT MY OWN COPY OF THE THEATER BOOK—SORT OF

A few days later, Mom got all excited when she told me she'd ordered a copy of the theater book online and it came in the mail.

"I got it used," she said. "So it was super cheap."

It was also, I discovered, highlighted to death. And someone had covered practically all the white space with notes.

Mom tried to find a silver lining. "Hey. At least you'll know what's important!"

I wanted to say *I don't want a stupid used book. I want a new one. It's not fair that Dad lost his job and college is so expensive.*

Instead I said, "Thanks." And then I shoved the book under my bed when she wasn't looking.

THE GLASS SLIPPERS

It's never too early to start thinking about props and costumes," Mrs. Delany said at rehearsal on Thursday.

She produced her neon-pink clipboard. "I'll be sending out an email to your families soon, but here are a few of the trickier items that we need. So peel open those peepers and start looking."

Mrs. Delany read off about a dozen things. She was super excited when Cameron said his dad was a mail carrier and would probably let us borrow one of his uniforms. And Andrea's family lived out in the country and she offered to bring in a butter churn and some other farm stuff for the set to make it look authentic. It was too bad the only interesting thing we had around our house was a giant box of throat swabs that Mom brought home when the hospital changed brands, and an old-fashioned phone that you dialed by putting your finger in a plastic spinner and turning it.

"Now, this is a long shot," Mrs. Delany said. "I'd really love it if we could find some glass slippers for Paige. I know the ball is in a barn, but I still want to pay homage to the original *Cinderella*. Real glass or clear plastic shoes may not work because they won't be visible from the audience, so I'm open to suggestions. What would look like glass?"

"What about covering some shoes with foil?" someone suggested. (Paige wrinkled her nose.)

Annie raised her hand. "I might have something that'll work."

"Really? Please share," Mrs. Delany said.

"My mom has a pair of character shoes with silver sequins on them. She wore them one year for Halloween when she dressed up as Dorothy from *The Wizard of Oz*."

"Dorothy's shoes were red," someone said.

"Not in the book," Mrs. Delany explained. "Red ones were used because they'd show up better on film."

I didn't know that. But Annie must have, because she beamed. "I'm not sure what size they are, but her feet aren't that big. And the sequins would sparkle like glass does."

"Wonderful!" Mrs. Delany exclaimed. Then she asked Paige to get together with Annie to work on the details.

I didn't understand why Annie was willing to help Paige out after she'd been mean to me. And apparently Paige wondered the same thing.

"The last time we talked, you were making accusations and demanding apologies," I overheard Paige tell Annie after rehearsal. "I'm kind of surprised you stepped up."

Annie shrugged. "It's for the good of the show."

Paige slowly nodded. "I respect that," she said. "So. Can you bring them next week?"

Annie promised she would start looking for them right away. I thought *right away* was a bit overboard. But I guess, like Annie said, it was for the good of the show.

NOTE TO SELF: DON'T TRUST THE "POPCORN" BUTTON ON THE MICROWAVE

I used the spare key to unlock the door. When I got inside, I hung it back on the hook near the kitchen sink. It was kind of a pain to remember to take it, but Mom said she didn't trust me to have my own key.

I let Bear out and finished up the last bit of math homework I had. There was a marathon of *Family Feud*, so I watched that for a while. I wasn't supposed to do homework with the TV on, but what Mom and Dad didn't know wouldn't hurt them, right? (At least that's what Sam said when I caught him sneaking a soda before dinner.)

Everything was going great until I wanted a snack.

I popped in one of those single-serving popcorn packets and pushed the button. But then Bear started whining to go out again. "You've got a bladder the size of a bumblebee bat's," I told her. (FYI: They're one of the smallest mammals in the world. I learned about them in third grade.)

It was sprinkling, so I had to go out with Bear because she doesn't like having wet feet. I guess I got distracted and lost track of time, because I was standing in the middle of the yard when I heard a faint *beep beep beep*.

I headed in, thinking the popcorn was ready, but it was the smoke alarm instead!

The kitchen was filled with smoke. First I tried waving my arms about to clear it, but that didn't do anything. Bear barked and jumped around my feet, adding to the noise. The back door was still open. What if the neighbors could hear the alarm and called the fire department?

I could feel panic rising with each beep of the alarm. The only way to quiet it was to clear the smoke. I opened all the windows. Then I grabbed a dish towel and started fanning the smoke detector to clear the air around it. A minute or two later, it finally shut off.

I guess I handled it well, but there was no hiding the disaster. Mom smelled the burnt popcorn the second she walked in. "What happened? Where were you? Why weren't you watching it?"

Unfortunately, this wasn't the last of the interrogation, either. Mom spent the whole night quizzing me between making dinner and clearing the dishes.

"What would you do if there was a fire?"

"What do you do if the electricity goes out?"

"What would you do if you didn't feel good?"

"What if you got hurt?"

"What would you do if someone tried to break in?"

"What if there was a storm and the tornado sirens went off?"

"What if you got a scary phone call?"

"Trick question," I said to that last one. "I'm not supposed to answer the phone."

There were a billion questions. I was surprised she didn't ask me what I'd do if a meteorite hit the city. And anytime Mom wasn't satisfied with my response, she'd go over a step-by-step plan of action.

"I got it," I told her. "Don't worry."

"I'm a mom," she said. "It's my job."

I thought about saying *"I'm a kid, it's my job to grow up."* But I decided that probably wasn't a good idea.

WWSCD?

Master Kim waited.

I stepped up to the practice paddle and got into fighting stance. There was a line of white and yellow belts behind me, so I took a quick breath before throwing my hammer fist.

"Huuup!"

My fist landed on the pad. It felt solid, but Master Kim said, "Do you think that would have broken the board?"

Whenever Master Kim asked you if you thought your technique was good or if you would have broken the board, the answer was usually no.

"Keep working," he said. "Visualize the board breaking."

I went to the back of the line and waited to try again. But class ended before I got a chance.

On the way home, I closed my eyes and tried what Master Kim had said.

"Are you falling asleep?" Dad teased.

"I'm visualizing my board break," I explained.

"That's a great idea. I learned in my psychology class that that's really helpful. Did you know—"

"Dad. It's hard to concentrate while you're talking."

"Oops. My B." It was funny when Dad tried to sound like a teenager. I hoped his future students would give him credit for trying.

I closed my eyes again, visualizing the entire board break. I started with standing in front of everyone and the judges. Then I imagined myself getting ready, staring down the board. I thought about how my arm would move and tried imagining how the edge of my hand would feel. The sound of the board cracking. The whiff of pine in the air. The board splinters on the ground. I imagined Master Kim bowing and handing me the pieces of the board. And me saying "*Thank you, sir.*"

Then I imagined having to ask for an ice pack.

"Sorry to interrupt," Dad said as we pulled into a parking lot, "but I need to stop at the grocery store to pick up something for dinner. Wanna run in with me or wait in the car?"

I followed Dad in.

On one of the end-of-the-aisle displays there was a sale on cake mixes.

"Oh, I *love* marble cake," Dad said. "Will you make one for dessert?" He didn't even wait for my answer, he just grabbed a box off the shelf and threw it in the basket.

After dinner, I got everyone out of the kitchen. ("An artist needs to focus!") I hadn't baked or decorated a cake in a long time. It felt good to measure and crack eggs and mix the batter. I used the fancy wooden spoon that Mom bought me at the farmers market.

Marble cake was new to me. Turns out you had to mix a portion of the cake batter with a packet of chocolate flavoring. And then you dropped dollops of brown batter into the yellow batter and swirled them together using a knife.

Swirling was so much fun that I got a little carried away. In the end, it looked less "marbled" and more like a light brown batter with a few stripes of white. I wasn't super happy, but oh well. You can't un-mix a cake.

I popped the pan in the oven and half an hour later, the whole house smelled delicious. Dad came into the kitchen as I got ready to take the cake out and turn it over on a plate to decorate it. I used a sheet-cake pan, so it was a little tricky getting the whole thing out. Well, okay, a little tricky is an understatement. Only half the cake came off. The other half got stuck in the pan. I had to pull it out with my hands.

"Did you flour the pan?" Dad asked.

Nerts. I forgot. I shook my head.

Instead of having one nice, rectangular cake, I had two halves with jagged sides. And they were a weird brown color.

"Now what?" I wondered out loud.

"WWSCD?" Dad responded. "What would Sweet Caroline do?"

I stood, hands on my hips, staring at the two pieces of cake on the counter. *Hmmm.*

I wasn't sure what Sweet Caroline would do. She'd probably start over. But I didn't have time. Besides, the cake tasted fine. It just looked a little broken. . . .

"What's the smile for?" Dad asked me.

"You'll see," I told him.

A little while later, I presented my "broken board" cake.

I may not be able to break a board at my test, I thought, *but at least I can bake one.*

STAGE DIRECTIONS

News flash. "Blocking" means something different in theater than it does in taekwondo. In taekwondo it means fending off a punch or kick. But in theater it's a fancy way of describing how actors move and do things onstage while they're saying their lines.

That's what we worked on at Tuesday's rehearsal.

"Which direction is upstage, again?" I whispered to Annie. The two of us were watching the people onstage stumble through the first act.

"That way," Annie whispered back, and pointed.

At the beginning of rehearsal, Mrs. Delany had given a big demonstration about stage directions. Where the audience sat was called "the house." The part of the stage closet to the house was called "downstage." And the part that I thought should be called the back of the stage was called "upstage." There was "center stage" (pretty easy to remember) and "stage left" and "stage right," too. They were based on you facing toward the audience. So stage left was to the audience's right. And stage right was to the audience's left. The tricky part was that even if you turned around, with your back to the audience, stage right and stage left didn't change.

If you ask me, it was perfectly reasonable that I was confused.

By the time we got to Act Three, we only had fifteen

minutes left, but Mrs. Delany wanted to let everyone have a little bit of time to block.

"We'll do more and more blocking as rehearsals progress," she explained. "But for now, everyone in the party scene, you stand upstage, center and stage right."

JJ and Vivian and I got directed toward the front of the group.

Mrs. Delany set the scene. "Now, the party is just revving up. The music is playing, but no one is dancing yet. And then there's a knock on the door."

Since we didn't have a set yet, Dave, who was playing the mailman who didn't get invited to the party even though he delivered all the invitations, pretended to knock. (Don't feel too bad for him; he gets invited in later on.)

"Hello?" Dave called out.

The script called for everyone to nominate my character to go see who it was.

Mrs. Delany motioned for me to walk across the stage to the pretend door. I was supposed to peek through the peephole (which wasn't there). Doing this was weird because Dave was just standing *right there*. But thankfully he looked down at his script so the two of us weren't eyeball to eyeball.

I tiptoed back to the group and stage-whispered, "It's Mr. Hatcher." The instant I said my line, someone's cell phone went off. The ringtone was a popular hip-hop song.

"Kill the music," I ad-libbed. "We're not supposed to be home."

Everyone cracked up. And the ringtone wasn't the only thing that made me feel like dancing.

As we gathered our things to go, I noticed Annie didn't seem to be in a very good mood. Maybe she was just tired. Best friends cheered each other when they were down, so I decided to ask her about the stage directions again. When white belts asked me about something I knew and they didn't it always made me feel better.

"So. Which way is downstage?" I asked her.

Annie gave a dramatic sigh and smiled. Then she grabbed my hand and used her pen to draw the diagram that Mrs. Delany showed us earlier.

"There. So you won't forget!" she said.

I stared at the diagram. It was in permanent ink! Mom hated when Sam wrote on himself. And what would Master Kim think if he saw it peeking out of my *dobok?*

I looked up. Annie was still smiling. Complaining would hurt her feelings.

"Thanks," I said.

WHEN I GOT HOME THAT AFTERNOON

"Mooom. Where's the rubbing alcohol?" I called down from the top of the stairs.

Instead of answering, Mom came up and found me rummaging through the bathroom drawers.

"Why do you need the rubbing alcohol?" she asked.

"Uh. For a school thing." (It was sort of the truth. Annie wrote on my arm in permanent marker while we were *at school*.)

"What school thing?"

"Can't tell you."

"Can't? Or don't want to?"

"The second one," I admitted.

Mom stood there. Waiting. There was no point in trying to make something up. Mrs. Delany may have liked my improv skills, but Mom wouldn't.

I pulled up my sleeve.

"Annie did it," I quickly explained about the diagram of the stage directions. "But I went online and it said rubbing alcohol will take it off."

Mom's mouth pulled into a thin line. After what felt like forever, she nodded. "Yep," she said. "Rubbing alcohol should take care of most of it. I've got some in my bathroom. Grab the cotton balls."

I did what she said and followed her down the hall. Then the two of us sat on the edge of the bathtub in my parents' bathroom.

"You're not mad?" I asked her as she doused a cotton ball. The rubbing alcohol made my eyes water.

"I'm not thrilled," she said. "But you thought it through and researched solutions. *And* you asked for help when you needed it. I'm proud of you for that."

Huh. All I did was ask where the rubbing alcohol was.

"You had a problem and handled it," Mom went on. "You're growing up."

"Thanks for noticing," I said. I wasn't trying to be a smart aleck, but Mom called me one anyway. She was smiling, though.

This wasn't like the "kitchen sink talks" we used to have (because we talked about everything but the kitchen sink), but it was nice. Mom and I didn't get to hang out much now that she had to work more hours. In fact, the last time I could remember having a mother-daughter outing was when we went shopping at the mall over the summer. But our day was cut short when Mom got called in to work at the last minute.

"Mom. You asked your boss for opening night off, right?" I asked.

"Yep."

"And Dad and Sam will be able to come, too?" I said.

"I'll drag them kickin' and screamin' if I have to!"

WALKING TACOS WEDNESDAY

It was almost time to leave for taekwondo.

"Oh, sorry," Dad said when he found me putting on my shoes and grabbing my bag. "I forgot to tell you, no class tonight."

"It got canceled?" I asked.

"No, but we're having company for dinner. You'll have to miss class." So *that* was why Mom had come home early.

"But I have my test coming up next month," I said. "I have to get ready!"

"Missing one class isn't a big deal. You can practice at home over the weekend. I'll help if you want."

It wouldn't be the same. I yanked my shoes off and threw them in the shoe bin. Then I stomped upstairs to change out of my T-shirt.

"What are you so mad about?" Sam asked me when I ran into him in the upstairs hallway.

"I have to miss taekwondo because Mom and Dad are having some stupid dinner guest!"

"Hey, watch it. That stupid dinner guest is my girlfriend."

Great. Just great! I had to miss preparing for my gold-belt test for *Megan*? I slammed my bedroom door and didn't answer when Sam knocked.

"You better not be this grumpy when she gets here," Sam said through the closed door.

This whole thing was so unfair! Taekwondo was way more important than dinner with Megan. Why did *my* plans have to be ruined? When I turned sixteen, I was going to get my driver's license right away. Maybe even before I ate cake and opened presents. That way, I could do what I wanted, whenever I wanted.

Even though I wasn't supposed to, I texted Annie.

That stinks, she texted back.

I know right? I texted.

Hey. Can we talk about this tomorrow? Kinda busy

I sent her a smiley emoji.

Sorry, she texted.

I was disappointed that Annie had to go. But at least it felt satisfying that I'd broken the rules about texting. Mom and Dad owed me, right? Still, I hoped they didn't notice when the phone bill came.

Half an hour later, Mom came to tell me dinner was ready and that she expected me to join them. I'd calmed down. But only a little bit.

"I hope you like tacos!" Mom said to Megan.

"Oh, I love tacos," Megan said. "The concession stand sells walking tacos on game nights. Sometimes they're out of them by third quarter, though."

I hadn't been to many games (crowds weren't really me and Dad's thing), but I knew the marching band got to take the third quarter off to walk around and get food.

Before coming downstairs, I had made a vow not to talk to Megan if I could help it.

I couldn't help it.

"What's a walking taco?" I asked.

Megan flashed a smile. "Oh, they are ahh-mazing! It's when you put meat and cheese and lettuce and sour cream inside a crushed bag of corn chips," she explained. "You carry it around and eat it with a fork."

"It sounds good," I admitted.

"It's pure junk food," Mom said. She was smiling but Sam still shot her a look anyway. That's another thing about having a mom who's a nurse. You're always in danger of getting lectures about the importance of fruits and vegetables.

"Sam says you're going to school to become a teacher," Megan said to Dad.

Dad beamed. "Yep. Just started my second year."

"What do you want to teach?"

"I'm leaning toward middle school. Probably social studies."

Middle school? That's the first time I've heard that.

"That's so awesome," Megan told him, like he'd announced he planned to cure cancer. "I might want to teach someday."

"Megan helped with the summer camps at the community center," Sam said. "And she helps with her church's summer Bible school."

"Well, that's terrific," Dad said. "Good for you."

I resisted the urge to roll my eyes. But just barely. Couldn't Dad see how she was only trying to get on his good side?

Mom asked me to get some more napkins. On the way back, I dropped a few and leaned down to pick them up. That's when I peeked under the table and saw Megan and Sam holding hands!

Ick. How weird was that? I mean, I guess they probably kissed. But I never thought about it.

We spent the next ten minutes talking about random stuff, like the upcoming marching-band trip and how Megan liked the smell of coffee but not the taste. I knew Mom was dying to tell her that teenagers shouldn't drink coffee, but she kept smiling and nodding like Megan was the best thing since tongue depressors.

Sam had just polished off his fourth taco when he suddenly pulled out his phone. "Oh man, we better get going," he said to Megan.

"Go where?" Mom asked.

"Megan and I are going over to Sanjay's house. Some people are getting together to plan the Fall Semiformal."

"I'm on the committee," Megan added.

Mom's smile grew wider. "That's lovely."

Uh-oh. Whenever Mom says "lovely" you should probably cut your losses and run. Mom turned to Sam. "And you're going, too?" she asked him.

Sam shrugged. "They're my friends."

"But you don't have a way there," Mom pointed out. "Or back."

Sam looked at her like she'd grown antlers. "Megan's taking me. She can bring me back."

Mom and Sam locked eyes.

"So Megan is going to drive you over to Sanjay's and then bring you back here, and then drive herself home? That sounds like a lot of driving for poor Megan."

"I . . . I don't mind," Megan said. "Really."

"Not tonight," Mom told Sam.

"Why?" he demanded.

"Because I said so."

"That's lame!"

Dad jumped in. "It's good he's getting involved," he said to Mom.

Mom whipped her head in Dad's direction. "It's a school night."

"It's only for a couple of hours," he countered.

The room grew so quiet that we could hear the wall clock tick. "He has homework," Mom said firmly.

"Not that much," Sam argued.

Neither Mom nor Dad looked in his direction. They were locked in a staring match. I wondered who would blink first.

Dad swallowed hard and turned to Sam. "Your mom's right. I'm sure the dance committee can handle things on their own."

It was two against one, and my brother knew it.

"This is messed up!" he said, shoving himself away from the table.

Megan quickly dabbed her mouth with her napkin and stood up. "Thanks for dinner," she said, looking uncomfortable.

"Can I at least walk her out to her car?" Sam asked sarcastically.

"Can you at least remember to be respectful to your mother?" Mom countered.

Sam growled and Mom began grabbing dishes off the table. Dad got up to help. But the second I could, I ducked outta there.

THINGS I THOUGHT OF WHEN I WAS HIDING OUT IN MY ROOM AND PAINTING MY TOENAILS:

1) Sam never used to act like that.
2) I wish Mom and Dad argued less.
3) If Dad's boss hadn't "downsized" him, Dad wouldn't be going to school, Mom wouldn't have to work so many shifts, money wouldn't be tight, and Mom and Dad wouldn't be so stressed out. This was all stupid Mr. Spencer's fault.
4) I still wanted to try walking tacos sometime.

OPENING NIGHT = OPPORTUNITY

At bedtime, Mom came to kiss me good night. "Hi, kiddo," she said, sitting down on the edge of my bed. "I wanted to apologize for dinner."

"It's okay."

Mom gave me a weary smile. "It's nice of you to let me off the hook, but I should have handled things better."

"Sam wasn't helping," I told her.

"No. He wasn't. But I'm the adult."

I wondered if she was going to apologize to Sam, too. Not that I thought she should. Sam didn't have to be so grumpy. On the other hand, I guess it *was* kinda mean of Mom to talk to him like that in front of Megan. I wouldn't like it if I got yelled at in front of my friends.

"So, let's change the subject. How's the play going?" Mom asked.

"Good."

"Do you have all your lines memorized yet?"

"Yep," I told her. "I don't have that many, so it wasn't hard."

"Excellent! Hey, if I haven't mentioned it lately," Mom said, "I'm really proud of you for stepping out of your comfort zone."

"Thanks."

"I like watching my kids perform," Mom said, tucking in my feet even though I was way too old for that. "It makes me happy."

I like watching my kids perform. It makes me happy.

I'd heard Mom say that before. When was it? Oh yeah. After Sam's Youth Orchestra show. It was on a Saturday night. Mom, Dad, and I got all dressed up. Sam wore his new black tux. (The boys in the orchestra wore tuxes. The girls wore long black dresses.) The show wasn't until eight o'clock, so we went out to a steak house beforehand. The place was so fancy that it had butter pats in the shape of flowers! We all drank water from these crystal goblets, too. We had the best time, talking and toasting and clinking our glasses.

After the show, we met up with Sam in the lobby of the theater. Mom gave him a "bouquet" of candy bars, and Dad made sure to order a CD recording of the show.

It was a great night. No one was fighting or stressed out. Everyone was happy. And we were together. I missed that.

Wait!

"Mom. Can we go out to dinner before my play?"

"I suppose so," she said.

"Maybe to that steak house we ate at before Sam's thing that one time?"

Mom frowned. "That might be a little out of our price range these days, but we could find somewhere else nice, I'm sure."

"Thanks," I told her.

"Sure thing," Mom said. "Good night."

After she left, I lay in bed, staring at the ceiling.

If we could just have one fun night together, maybe we'd all remember we like each other and things would start to get better.

Opening night would be the perfect opportunity.

THE NEXT DAY

I caught Annie on the way out of homeroom. "Wanna practice lines at lunch?" I asked her.

"It's called 'running lines,'" she informed me.

"Okay. Wanna run lines then?"

Annie smiled. "Absol-totally!"

I must have looked confused.

"Sorry! Paige says that. It's fun, right?"

"Have you and Paige been hanging out?" I asked.

"Oh, uh. We were in her backyard last night," she said, shifting her books from one arm to the other. "Well. She was in her backyard and I was in mine."

Was that the reason Annie had texted that she had to go? Was she *with* Paige when she and I had been texting? It felt like someone had socked me in the stomach.

"I saw that she was outside," Annie was saying. "So I walked over the pair of silver shoes. I think they're going to be perfect, by the way! Isn't that great?"

I nodded, but Annie didn't notice my heart wasn't in it.

"Anyway, she told me again how she respected that I shared the shoes even though I'd been upset with her. And we got to talking. I told her I wanted to be an actor, too. She said she'd give me a few tips and that we could 'talk shop.' Isn't that cool?"

Best friends are happy for each other.

"Absol-totally," I told her.

WAR

Greetings and salutations, friends," Mrs. Delany said, motioning for us to find a seat. It was time for our pre-rehearsal pep talk.

Annie wanted to sit with Paige. "She waved us over," she said. First off, I was pretty sure she meant it for Annie, not me. And secondly, if you asked me, Annie was a little too gung ho about Paige mentoring her. But a *best* best friend would be supportive.

"You go," I told her.

Annie chewed her bottom lip. "Are you sure?" I nodded and then sat down with JJ and Vivian on the opposite side of the stage.

"Just a friendly reminder," Mrs. Delany said. "I expect you all to be off-book in five days. That's approximately one hundred and twenty hours from now. Please plan accordingly." Next, she called for the actors in the second act.

This bugged me. I liked for things to go in order. In baking, you had to follow the steps of a recipe. Taekwondo was like that, too. We always started class by bowing in and then doing meditation. But Mrs. Delany did things out of order. Instead of doing the play from start to finish, she'd have us rehearse whatever scene she felt needed work. Or based on who was at rehearsal. I tried my best not to think about it too much, or how Annie didn't hesitate when I told her to sit with Paige.

If you weren't onstage, you were supposed to either watch your fellow performers or occupy yourself quietly. JJ, Vivian, and I played a three-way version of War in the wings with a deck of cards we'd found. (FYI: The "wings" were the parts of the stage off to the sides. That's where you waited to go on or went after you left the stage. You couldn't see them from the audience.)

Annie and Paige were in the wings on the other side of the stage, watching the scene and taking notes. "*Wanna play?*" I mouthed when I looked over and caught Annie's eye.

Annie smiled, looked at Paige, and then shook her head. She motioned for me to join them.

I tossed my cards down in the draw pile. "I'm going to go watch the scene," I told JJ and Vivian.

"It's copacetic," JJ said. Vivian rolled her eyes. She'd asked him what that word meant the first time he'd said it. Apparently it was some old slang word that was kind of like saying "cool."

I tiptoed backstage and around to the other side, where Annie and Paige were, and sat down.

"Hey," Annie said when I joined them. "You finish your game?"

"It's still going," I told her. "I just thought I'd see what you guys were doing."

"*We're* paying attention to the work onstage," Paige said.

"It's important to study your craft," Annie explained. Craft? Boy. She was taking acting seriously. But that was fair. After all, I studied baking by watching shows and reading cookbooks. And I spent a lot of time thinking about stuff Master Kim taught us. Annie was serious about this and if Operation BBF was going to succeed, I had to take it seriously, too.

"So, what are we supposed to be watching for?" I asked.

Paige rolled her eyes. It was Annie who answered. "We're seeing who's listening and who's waiting."

"Huh?"

"A good actor listens to the dialogue and responds. They don't just wait for their turn to talk."

I nodded like I understood. "Ah. Got it."

We continued watching. Annie and Paige scribbled down a few notes. "Hmm, interesting choice," Paige murmured about someone. Annie agreed.

I had no idea what they were talking about. I tried asking a few more questions, but Paige kept sighing, and

Annie smiled but put her finger to her lips. What was the deal? *She* was the one who invited me over.

I gave up and went back to the card game.

"You'll have to wait till we finish this round," Vivian said apologetically.

"Nah," JJ said, scooting over to make room for me. "You can take half of my stack."

"Oooo, half the stack," Vivian teased. "Must be true love."

I couldn't be a hundred percent sure, but I think JJ blushed.

A LITTLE SURPRISE

A couple of days later, Mom called me into the kitchen when she got home.

"I got you something today," she said. She reached into her purse and pulled out a small brown bag. "Pretend it's wrapped with a bow."

I smiled and then slipped my hand inside.

It was a key!

"I figured it would be easier if you had your own key, since you're going to be staying by yourself some afternoons," Mom explained. "I think there's a carabiner in the junk drawer," she went on. "You can attach it to a hook inside your backpack. Pockets aren't always reliable."

A key. To the house. That was mine.

I wrapped my arms around Mom and squeezed. "Thank you," I told her.

I was ready for her to give me a lecture about what a big responsibility this was and how I'd better keep track of it and not make her regret trusting me. But all Mom did was hug me back and say, "You're welcome."

COMMERCIAL GIRL

I met up with Annie at her locker on Monday and handed her my flash cards with the Korean words I needed to memorize. She wanted to help me get ready for my gold-belt test, which I thought was nice of her. Maybe she was trying to make it up to me for *shhhing* me when I tried to ask her and Paige questions at rehearsal. We only had about ten minutes before the first bell, but Annie said a minute here and a minute there could add up.

"How do you count to twenty?" she asked. I counted for her and she laughed. "Okay. I guess I'll have to take your word for it."

She flipped to the next card. "What does"—she sounded the word out—"*choonbi* mean?"

"It's *choon*-bee," I said.

"That's what I said."

"You said *choon*-bye."

Annie giggled. "Sorry. Okay what does *choon-beee* mean?"

"Ready position," I told her. I knew I was right, but she checked the back of the card and nodded.

"Who's getting ready?" a voice behind us said.

Annie and I turned around and found Monica (the girl who played the Dairy Godmother) and Paige there.

Annie's face lit up. "Hi guys!"

"Hey Annie," Paige said.

"Hi," I said. Monica smiled, but Paige didn't say anything.

"So. Who's getting ready for what?" Monica repeated.

"Oh. Annie's just helping me with my memorization," I told her.

"Good idea," Paige said. "We're off-book this week."

I knew that. *Everyone* knew that. Mrs. Delany had reminded us a billion times.

"It's for her belt test," Annie explained to Paige.

"I do taekwondo," I added.

Paige scoffed. "My older *brother* does that. He's a brown belt."

"Um. That's cool. There are lots of girls in my class, too," I blurted out. I didn't want her to think martial arts was only for boys.

Paige looked at me like I was wearing roller skates. "Good for you and your class," she said. Then she turned to Annie.

"I took a stage weapons class over the summer. You should look into it."

"Really? That sounds awesome," Annie said.

"Yeah, it was fun. We learned how to do fake sword and knife fights. Plus, the more special skills you have on your acting résumé, the better."

Special skills. Résumé. *Hummph.* Paige was acting like she was a major movie star instead of an eighth grader who did one lousy commercial. And Annie was buying it!

"We should keep practicing," I said to Annie. She gave me a look that I couldn't quite figure out.

"Don't let me keep you," Paige said. "If you have better things . . ."

Annie's smile looked like it was hurting her. "No, no. It's not that. I just promised Eliza I'd study with her."

"Later," Paige said. She and Monica faded into the sea of kids hurrying to their homerooms.

Since the bell was about to ring, Annie handed back the flash cards. The two of us headed down the hall. "That was a little rude," she said.

"It was?"

Annie sighed. "Paige is helping me. Will you please be nice to her?"

"I *was* nice!"

Annie looked at me.

A best friend is honest. "She started it," I said.

"What are you talking about?"

"When we did our character developments and she said my character's embarrassing moment should be getting caught in the shower."

Annie was confused. "Are you still mad about *that*? I think she was just trying to help."

"Why are you defending her?"

"I'm not."

"Yes, you are," I said.

Annie sighed.

"I thought you said you'd always be on my side," I added.

"I *am* on your side," Annie said. "Don't you believe me?"

"I guess," I told her. But I didn't.

CUE LINES

Toward the end of Tuesday's rehearsal, Monica and Paige were doing the scene where the Dairy Godmother (Monica) visits Cinder Ellen (Paige) and whips up a dress for her to wear to the Barnyard Bash.

Monica was supposed to wave a pencil (the wand would come later) and say her magic spell. Only she just stood there.

"Oh, no," Annie whispered next to me. "She forgot her line!"

I knew what it felt like to have everyone waiting on you. Like at my yellow-belt test when I couldn't remember *charyut* meant "attention." And that was only in front of a few judges.

Paige stared at Monica. The seconds dragged on.

Finally, Mrs. Delany gave Monica the line. Monica's shoulders relaxed and she repeated the spell. She said a few more lines. But then she stopped again. Paige and Monica just stood there.

Something was wrong. What were they waiting for?

Fifteen seconds or so later, Anthony, the boy who played the goat who got turned into the tractor driver (who drove Cinder Ellen to the party), stepped onstage. He looked confused.

Mrs. Delany stopped the scene and called for everyone's attention. "Eyes and ears on me, fellow thespians," she said. "This is very important, so write it down in your scripts."

Everyone grabbed their scripts and pencils. Normally we just wrote down notes that Mrs. Delany gave us about how to do a scene. But sometimes she gave us general feedback or advice.

Mrs. Delany waited until our pencils were poised. "First of all, we are off-book. You must know and live and breathe your lines. And second, there's a reason you must memorize your lines exactly as they were written. And it's not because the playwright is awesome. Even if the playwright is me this time around." Mrs. Delany smiled and batted her eyes to let us know she didn't take herself too seriously.

She went on. "One of my veterans, please explain to the new folks what a 'cue line' is."

Paige didn't even raise her hand; she just started talking. "A cue line is a line that prompts an action. For example, another actor making an entrance or dropping a book onstage or something like that. It can also direct the crew to make a sound effect or turn on a spotlight."

I bet Paige knew a lot about spotlights.

"Thank you, Paige," Mrs. Delany said.

"So, Monica was supposed to say a line that signaled Anthony to come onstage?" I asked Annie.

"Yeah. She didn't give him his cue. That's why he got confused."

Mrs. Delany cleared her throat. "Everyone repeat after me: Cue lines are crucial."

Everyone repeated the line.

"Again!" Mrs. Delany sang.

"*Cue lines are crucial.*"

She gave us the "okay" sign and then looked at the clock. "All right, friends. Time to scoot your boots!"

KICHO EE BO CHA CHA CHA

It was chilly at the community center on Wednesday night. I was glad I wore a long-sleeved shirt under my *dobok*. The stage at school was usually hot. I felt like Goldilocks because it was hard to find clothes that were "just right" for both places.

I liked being busy, but doing taekwondo and the play was tough. Homework piled up and I ended up doing it in the car or on the bus. And I had a bunch of episodes of *Sweet Caroline Cakes* to catch up on. On top of that, I was tired, which made it extra hard to concentrate.

After warm-ups, Master Kim divided us into groups to work on *poomsae*, or "forms." Forms were a way to practice kicking and punching with an imaginary opponent. They needed a lot of concentration. When I was a white belt, my form was called *kicho il bo*. The name meant "basic form No. 1," which was boring. So I added *cha cha cha* in my head because then it sounded like a dance.

My new form was called *kicho ee bo (cha cha cha)* and it meant "basic form No. 2." Which was a boring name, too. The later forms had more interesting meanings, like "great principle of heaven," or "great principle of happiness."

Kicho ee bo wasn't too hard to learn. That's because it followed the same I-shaped pattern that my first form had.

I didn't get the whole pattern thing at first. But one day Master Kim pulled out these plastic disks and laid them out on the ground in the shape of capital I. When he did the form, I could see how it traced the lines.

Master Kim called the yellow belts to the center of the room so we could practice. "*Shijak!*" (That meant "Begin.")

I went over the steps in my head:

Turn to the left, face block in front stance.

Step, still front stance, face punch . . .

When we were done, Master Kim said, "*Bah ro,* return to starting position. *Shool,* rest."

Everyone turned around to face the front, bowed, and stood at attention.

"Nice job. I saw several strong front stances." I wondered if he was talking about mine. "We are going to go through the form again. This time, I want you to show me your best effort. Imagine you are at your test."

This time, the white, gold, and orange belts and the black-belt helpers sat along the wall to watch. My heart picked up a little, but I focused on my stance. (Just in case he hadn't been talking about mine earlier.)

I got through the beginning and the middle just fine. But when I got to the second-to-last turn, I saw Master Kim out of the corner of my eye and my brain stopped working. I waited for my arms and legs to remember what to do, but they weren't much help, either. It took watching everyone else and stumbling around a bit to figure out what to do next.

Applesauce.

When we were done, Master Kim had us return to the starting position and wait at attention. My face felt warm. And not just from doing the form two times in a row.

"Remember," Master Kim said. "Always show confidence in a test, even if you may not feel it. If you make a mistake, keep going. Do not stop. Do not change your expression. Do not sigh or groan. It is possible your error won't be noticed as long as you do not draw attention to it."

Then Master Kim told us a story about how one of his older students went to a competition and completely messed up her form halfway through. But she didn't let her confidence break for a second and even made the same mistake on both sides so it looked like the form was *supposed* to be that way. Master Kim said she got first place—all because she was confident and had strong technique, even if it was the wrong technique.

"And guess who that student was," Master Kim said at the end. He used his hand to motion toward Miss Abigail.

"It's true," Miss Abigail said, blushing.

Even though the story had a surprise ending, and even though Master Kim wasn't looking at me, I was all kinds of confident he was talking to me because I had messed up. Here's another thing I was confident about: I was going to keep practicing my form. And my poker face.

NEXT REHEARSAL

The backstage area was floor-to-ceiling crammed with boxes and oversized props from old plays. (There was even a fully decorated Christmas tree.) But we couldn't stop to explore. Our group was headed to the costume closet.

There were six of us, including me and Annie. Mrs. Delany had been sending small groups to the closet each rehearsal. We were supposed to rummage around for things that might work for our costumes.

The backstage area was cool, but the costume closet was a thousand times better! Every nook and cranny was filled with clear plastic crates. Each crate was labeled:

HATS
SHOES (SIZES 5 TO 10)
SCARVES AND PURSES
JEWELRY
UNIFORM MEDALS
BOOTS

And the clothes! Racks and racks and racks of every type of clothing you could possibly think of. Coats, jackets, military uniforms, furry animal costumes, vintage dresses, marching-band uniforms, aprons, suits and tuxedos, and shirts that looked like they were from the future with silver metallic edging and pockets. (What kind of awesome show needed that outfit?) There was even a wedding dress! It was like the Room of Requirement. Only for outfits.

We started grabbing things and modeling them.

"Check these out! I think they're called go-go boots!"

"Ooo. Look what I found!"

"Lemme try it on."

After a while, Cole (the high-schooler who was our stage manager) popped his head in to check on us, and we started focusing on our costumes. Annie and I went to look at the party dresses. The Little Pigs were going to wear headbands with pink felt pig ears glued on—well, JJ was going to wear a baseball cap with felt pig ears—but I needed fancier clothes for the Barnyard Bash scene.

"Find anything?" Annie asked.

The two of us hadn't talked about our conversation on Monday. I was still hurt that Annie had said I was rude to Paige. But I wanted to stay friends with Annie more than I wanted to stay mad.

"What about this one?" she asked. She held up a blue dress with puffy sleeves. I rubbed the fabric between my fingers and then shook my head. Annie understood my deal with itchy clothes.

Even though there were half a dozen dresses that would have *looked* good for the party scene, I couldn't find one that would be comfortable enough to wear.

"We can keep looking," Annie said cheerfully. "Mrs. Delany said not to panic if we can't find something."

I appreciated that she was trying to keep me from getting discouraged.

"Let's look for something for you instead," I suggested.

We found a perfect ratty, oversized bathrobe right away. It was even green, Annie's favorite color. Afterward, we pulled out the WIGS container. The tile floor was a bit dirty, so we used a couple of suitcases we found in a corner as chairs.

Annie and I took turns trying on wigs and making up funny names of the people who'd wear them.

"Hey. I'm Stanley," Annie said in a deep voice as she adjusted a short, brown wig on her head.

I grabbed a long, blond wig. "I'm Sparkles O'Hara and I'm ready for my star on the Hollywood Walk of Fame!"

This went on for a while. Once we started adding funny accents, the two of us laughed so hard we could hardly breathe.

Cole came back in to give everyone a ten-minute warning, so Annie and I grabbed the bathrobe and went to return the suitcases. (None of the wigs were exactly what she was looking for to play the old-lady neighbor.)

"Hey," Annie said. "Careful. Your suitcase is unlatched."

The suitcase was one of those old-time ones made out of leather. I went to set it down so I could close it all the way. But as soon as I did, the lid fell open and a folded piece of paper fluttered out.

THE NOTE INSIDE THE SUITCASE

Hello!!

My name is Cecilia. I played the New York "Starlet" when we did the show Annie. This is the suitcase I got to carry when I sang "NYC." I thought it would be fun to hide this note where another actor might find it.

Here's my favorite theater joke: Why do people say "break a leg" before you go onstage? Because every play has a cast! haha

Anyway, I hope you liked my note! When you get to high school, come say "hi" if I'm still there.

Cecilia Simon

"I know her!" Annie said. "I saw her when I was little and my moms took me to see *The Sound of Music* at the high school. She was Maria."

That meant the note would have been written at least five years ago. Hadn't anyone opened this suitcase before now?

"Are you sure it was her?" I asked.

"Positive! She was a really good singer."

I knew Annie couldn't possibly know for sure if the actor she saw was Cecilia, but both of us really wanted it to be true. So we decided it was.

GOODWILL

On Saturday, Mom drove me and Annie to the Goodwill store. I was embarrassed we couldn't afford to buy something from the costume shop Mrs. Delany suggested. And that I had to buy a dress at a place where people donated things they didn't want anymore. But Annie tried to make me feel better.

"Goodwill is sooo much cooler," she said. "They'll have awesome vintage stuff. Plus, lots of people go bargain hunting and then post about their great finds online. They even write blogs about it."

I wanted to hug her.

There was a rack of Halloween costumes right inside the front door, so Annie and I stopped and checked it out while Mom wandered around the housewares shelves. ("There might be something we could add to the costume closet," Annie insisted.) There were even itty-bitty costumes for babies! Pumpkins, peas in a pod, a dragon. And a bumblebee. I swatted it away when Annie held it toward me, and we laughed. I had been scared of bees ever since I was four and one flew into my mouth and stung my tongue. Annie was the only person outside my family who knew that story. She was allowed to tease me about it.

When we didn't find anything in the costume section, Annie and I headed for the rack of old prom and party dresses against one of the walls.

"There *has* to be something that'll work," Annie said.

The two of us started on opposite ends and worked our way toward each other. Mrs. Delany had told us not to worry too much about sizes because she had a parent volunteer who could help hem and take things in.

Annie and I each found a few options for me to try on. My top choice was a dark blue dress. It was plain, no lace or buttons to mess with. It was also made of a slick material that felt soft. My favorite part of it, though, was that along the bottom hem it had a thin ribbon of gold. It seemed like a good omen since I was about to take my gold-belt test.

I took the six dresses Annie and I found to the changing room. Annie stayed outside and waited for me to model them. Each time I came out, she made a comment and then gave the dress a score.

"Eh. It's okay," she said about the first one. "But I don't like the color. I give it a four out of ten."

I saved the blue dress for last. None of the others had gotten higher than a seven on Annie's scale. Holding my breath, I tried it. It was perfect! And the best part was that it didn't itch or have any pinchy elastic.

Annie clapped her hands the second I stepped out. "Ten! Ten!"

I took a bow and Annie clapped harder and called, "Bravo!" People nearby glanced our way, but Annie didn't care. I loved how she was willing to make a spectacle of herself so I'd feel special.

I carefully put the blue dress back on its hanger and draped it over my arm.

"Now you," I told Annie.

We headed over to the shoe section. Finding the rest of her costume was super easy. In about thirty seconds flat, we found a pair of fuzzy slippers that looked like kittens, complete with whiskers. "They're perfect!" Annie said.

"Now all you need is an old-lady wig. I saw some by the front door," I told her.

Annie blinked. "Oh. I forgot to tell you. I think I already found one."

"You did?"

"Well, sort of. Paige said she probably had something I could use. I'm supposed to go over sometime this week and check it out."

"Oh."

Annie smiled. "Are you ready? Let's go find your mom."

WHAT MOM FOUND

Mom had an armful of stuff when we tracked her down. "Look what I found, Eliza!" she said, setting a couple of items on a nearby shelf so she could show me.

It was a large plastic bag with smaller frosting bags and a bunch of metal decorating tips inside!

"Holy cheese and crackers!" I said.

Mom beamed. "Great find, right? And look at the price." It was cheap enough that I could afford it.

Annie, Mom, and I headed to the counter to pay for our things. While Mom got out her wallet, I tallied up the events of the morning: I'd found out that Annie was still buddy-buddy with Paige. But I'd also found the perfect dress for my costume in the Barnyard Bash scene *and* I got some new cake-decorating tips. Maybe I'd try them out when I got home. Like Sweet Caroline said on one episode, "When life gives you lemons, make lemon cake!"

FYI

You actually need lemons to make a lemon cake. You can't just use yellow food coloring. And orange juice isn't a good substitute.

But don't ask me how I know this.

A LITTLE EXTRA OOMPH

The lemon cake didn't go so well, but I could still make lemonade. Metaphorically speaking.

On Sunday morning, I went to the basement and climbed into the crawl space. The box I was looking for was way in the back, and I kept having to pull away spiderwebs.

It took a bit of digging, but I finally found it: the wig Sam wore when the drum line dressed up for a talent show. It would be perfect for Annie!

I knew she said Paige might have one, but best friends surprise each other, right?

I took the wig upstairs and carefully brushed it out. It was blond, shoulder length, and it had just the right amount of curl at the ends. It was going to look great with rollers!

Now. To color it.

I knew painting wasn't going to work. I'd tried painting my Barbie doll's head once when I was little. All that happened was that it turned crunchy. *And* the paint chipped off after a while.

Would permanent marker work?

I searched the junk drawer: A deck of cards. A single shoelace. Old keys. Pipe cleaners. A toothbrush. Gray shoe polish. A rain poncho, a rubber-band ball, and a bunch of other random stuff. But no marker.

Hold the salt! The shoe polish!

After I laid a few layers of newspaper on the floor (I'd learned my lesson after the nail polish incident at the end of summer), I grabbed a pair of disposable vinyl gloves. Then I draped the wig over an old vase and got to work.

The shoe polish, which even came with its own built-in brush, went on smoothly. After a few coats, the wig looked pretty good if I did say so myself. It even had a nice silvery sheen to it that would stand out under the lights onstage.

But it was missing something . . . a little extra oomph. *Glitter!*

I rummaged around in the drawer where Mom kept her art stuff. (She used to do a lot of scrapbooking, back when she had more free time.) No one was allowed to use her good scissors, but I figured she wouldn't mind if I took some blue glitter. Annie's character was definitely the kind of old lady to have blue streaks in her hair.

Since the shoe polish wasn't quite dry, the glitter stuck to it like I was hoping it would. I carefully added a few electric-blue highlights here and there and tapped the excess glitter off onto the paper. It was a good thing I wore the gloves; the polish and glitter were all over.

When the wig seemed dry, I wrapped it in tissue paper and put it in a gift bag.

Annie was going to love it.

REHEARSAL BREAK ON TUESDAY

I love it!"

"Yay!" I told Annie. "I'm so glad. Are you surprised?"

"I can't believe you made this," she said. "You could totally be on the costume crew."

My heart felt like bursting. I was glad I'd decided to wait until the break to give Annie the wig. This way it was just the two of us. "You should try it on," I said.

"Come with!" Annie said, pulling me out the door.

Annie and I headed to the nearest bathroom. Standing in front of the mirror, Annie pulled her hair into a ponytail and tucked it inside the wig. It took a bit of wiggling but she got it on.

She smiled.

"Thank you!" she said. "I really love the blue highlights." She reached up to play with the hair.

"Aaaaah, oh no!" she said suddenly.

She pulled her hands off the wig and showed them to me. They were all silver. And blue.

"The paint is coming off," Annie said. She grabbed a paper towel and tried wiping her hands. It didn't work.

"What kind of paint is this?" she said, panicking.

"Uh. It's not paint," I told her. "It's shoe polish."

"Oh no, no, no. That stuff *never* comes out."

She blasted the faucet and tried scrubbing her hands with soap. It helped, but there was still gray polish and blue glitter stuck to her hands.

Annie began to cry a little. I felt terrible. I should've known better after so much stuff came off on the disposable gloves. I just figured once the polish dried, it'd be fine. "Don't touch your face," I told Annie, grabbing her hands away.

I got some toilet paper from a stall and wiped her tears. Then I used a paper towel to grab the wig and pull it off. "At least there isn't any on your head," I said. Annie sniffed.

"I'm sorry," I told her.

"I know you didn't mean it," Annie said. "But I can't go around with gray hands. I'm in my aunt's wedding this weekend. What am I gonna do?"

"Maybe it'll wear off by then," I suggested.

"Why didn't you think this through?"

Annie stared at me but I had no answer for her. We stood like that for a few seconds before the restroom door swung open.

In strolled Paige. "What's going on?"

Annie began sniffling again and showed Paige her hands. "No worries," Paige said. "An actor is always prepared."

Paige set her purse down and began rummaging through it. "This should do the trick," she said, pulling out a tub of something labeled COLD CREAM. "It's for removing stage makeup," Paige explained. I wanted to ask how often she went around wearing stage makeup, but this was an emergency.

Paige produced a baggie of cotton balls from her purse, too. Then she dabbed some cold cream on a cotton ball and began rubbing it in circles on Annie's hands. The gray and blue began coming off. It took a bunch of cotton balls and cold cream and rinsing, but Annie's hands were clean in the end.

Annie hugged Paige. "You're a lifesaver! Thank you, thank you, thank you."

"I'll go let Mrs. Delany know why you're late getting back from break," Paige said. On her way out, she shook her head in my direction.

Great. Annie was upset with me. Paige got to save the day. And now Mrs. Delany would know I'd done something stupid.

I tossed the wig back into the gift bag and then chucked them both in the trash can on the way out.

THE PART WHERE
I LEARN THE
IMPORTANCE OF
TAPPING OUT

At Wednesday's taekwondo class we practiced arm bars. Those are when you trap someone's arm and press on the back of it just above the elbow. It's not an attack. It's a way to control your opponent. When your arm started to hurt, you were supposed to tap out. Which meant lightly hit your own body, your attacker's body, or the ground a few times to let your partner know to stop.

"Go slowly," Master Kim called out.

Sophia wasn't there, so I partnered with an orange belt who was a foot taller than me. The first time he grabbed my arm and pressed, I fell to my knees. Obviously, he didn't pay attention to the directions.

Oww! "Okay! Stop!" I said.

"Sorry," my partner said, pulling me up. "I didn't feel you tap."

That's because my brain couldn't think anything else but oww, *dude.*

Master Kim slid over. "You have to protect your training

partner," he told the orange belt. "There is no learning without trust."

"Yes, sir," my partner said, and bowed.

Master Kim turned to me. "And you. You must clearly communicate with your partner."

Grimacing doesn't count? I thought but didn't say out loud.

"Tap out the moment you need to," Master Kim told me. "Better yet, *before* you need to. Protect yourself."

My partner practiced his arm bar on me again. This time, as soon as he started pressing on my arm, I hit the bottom of his leg a few times and he let me up.

Next, it was my turn to try doing the technique against my partner. He punched, and I stepped to my left at the same time I blocked his punch with my right hand. Then I quickly grabbed his wrist and turned it so his arm was locked straight. I followed that by stepping forward and using my left forearm to press on the back of his arm, just above his elbow. This caused him to lean over and fall to his knees.

My partner tapped the ground.

I reached out my hand to help pull him up. He rubbed his arm.

"You okay?" I said. "Did I do it wrong?"

"It's all right," he said. "And no. You got it."

The two of us practiced a few more times. We both got better at tapping out, but we still sometimes hurt each other without meaning to. It was surprising how fast it could go from okay to not okay.

"MY BOOTS ARE KILLING ME."

Agood martial artist communicates with their training partner. A best friend should communicate, too. So on Thursday at lunch, I apologized to Annie about the wig. Again.

"It all worked out," she said with a shrug. "I'm just grateful Paige was there to fix it."

I nodded. "Yeah. Me too." (*Not.*)

Annie set her milk down and looked at me. "But there is something I don't get," she said. "I told you Paige already had a wig for me."

"I wanted to surprise you," I said.

"Well, you did! And I guess it's the thought that counts."

I was relieved when Annie changed the subject. It wasn't an arm bar, but I wanted to tap out of the conversation.

"So, should we put in something about doing theater?" Annie asked, opening up our Rules to Surviving Sixth Grade notebook.

"Like what?"

"I dunno. How 'bout 'See a school play'?"

I didn't really see how that was a good survival tip, but best friends agree. "Maybe," I said.

Annie smiled. "Maybe, milady?"

I groaned but played along. "Dear sir, I regret I cannot dance. My boots are killing me."

These were lines from the play. The whole cast had been listening to each other say our lines for weeks now. And the new thing was to go around quoting each other. Even when we weren't in rehearsal.

"Maybe one of our tips should be 'Don't wear cowboy boots,'" I joked.

Annie cracked up.

This felt good. Hanging out and working on our Rules to Surviving list.

Annie crunched on a fat baby carrot. (Rules to Surviving Sixth Grade No. 19: The only acceptable lunch vegetables are ones you can eat with your hands.) It reminded me of the time Mom's work was throwing a party, and Mom spent days washing and peeling and cutting vegetables. She used them to make a "veggie skeleton." She said one of the other nurses brought "amputated toes," which were really just hot-dog pieces rolled in pizza dough. She'd even added ketchup for fake blood.

I wondered if I'd get a chance to go to a party this year. I'd been to classroom parties, of course. And a few birthday parties when I was younger and parents made the person give invites to everyone. That was before we knew I had ADHD. Tony knew about the ADHD, though, and I didn't get invited to his birthday party over the summer. He said it was because he thought I was mad at him. But I wasn't. I apologized and he apologized. It was the last time I talked to him. Sometimes I saw him in the halls. He'd give me a quick nod, and I'd nod back.

I heard there'd be a cast party after the play was over, after strike. "Strike," FYI, was when everyone got together to tear down the sets. Strike for *Cinder Ellen* was right after the closing show.

I was just about to ask Annie if she'd heard anything about where the cast party was going to be when someone nearby popped a chip bag. It startled the whole cafeteria into silence for a second, and then everyone burst out laughing. Well, except for the cafeteria monitor, who was headed over to the noise-maker's table.

"Hey," I said. "This barn is a-bustin' . . ."

Annie finished the line: "and this party is a-poppin'!"

She knew that one super well; it was the cue line Paige said so that Annie knew to come onstage in Act Three.

BARNYARD MUCK

My tailbone was aching. It did that sometimes since I'd hurt it over the summer. I got up to give it a break and get more paint.

Some people were complaining that the cast had to help paint the barn set. But I thought it was fun. And Mrs. Delany reminded everyone that a production is more than just being onstage. "A lot of cooperation and elbow grease go into every show!" she said.

I arched my back and accidentally dripped paint on JJ's head in the process. "Hey!" he protested.

"Sorry," I said.

"No problemo." It was another one of his old slang words. "You can drip on me anytime."

I know he was only being JJ, but it made my cheeks flush. What was with the blushing? Did I like JJ? Wait. Did he like *me*?

I headed over to where all the paint cans were laid out on a giant tarp. Annie came with. "There's no more brown," she said.

Stage manager Cole grabbed a can and starting pouring. "Just start mixing colors," he said. "It's a barn. It's okay if it's not perfect. In fact, it'll look better if it's not."

I took over the mixing, adding a little bit of this and a little bit of almost-out-of that. Sometimes, I mixed fingernail polish and created my own colors. But this was more fun because it was gallon-sized.

Annie grinned as I got carried away. "What color is that?" she asked.

"I call it Barnyard Mud!" I said.

Paige, who was off to the other side with the group painting the white picket fence, coughed once. "I call it Baby Poop," she said under her breath. The other kids laughed.

I ignored them and kept mixing. I felt like a mad

scientist or a wizard. Or even the Dairy Godmother about to cast a spell.

"Mimzy whimsy wahk-wollow-me flay," I said, pouring the contents of another can into the mixture. "Forces of the universe, bend my way."

Paige stood up, hands on her hips. "You're not allowed to say that! That's *Monica's* line!"

I startled. "What are you talking about?"

"Don't quote Monica's line. You're messing it up."

"No I'm not."

"Yes. You are! It's mimzy *muh*-whimsy. You're going to mess her all up if you keep saying it wrong. So stop it."

"It's okay," Monica told Paige.

"No. It's not," Paige said. "You're being too nice."

Everyone was watching. I don't know where Mrs. Delany had run off to. But Cole was putting lids back on the paint cans and pretending he wasn't listening.

Usually, I can think of too many things to say. But this time, my brain took a break. I hoped Paige was wrong. I didn't mean to mess up Monica. The play was important to me, too. It was the best way to be Annie's BBF. It was also a chance to get my whole family together and happy for one night.

Annie tugged my elbow. "Come on. Let's go finish the barn."

Once we got back to our painting spot, my mouth started working again. "What did I ever do to her?"

Annie shrugged. "She's worried about the play is all."

"Don't you think I care about how the play goes, too?" I asked her.

"Of course you do," Annie said. "Paige is just stressed out. She's the lead. Cut her some slack."

Toast on a raft.

JJ leaned over. "Paige is a diva," he said. "You know what that stands for, right? Dedicated to Issuing Vicious Attitude."

Vivian and I laughed. Annie gave us a weak smile but didn't say anything. And then we went back to painting.

I tried to shake it all off. But for the rest of the afternoon, Barnyard Mud looked more like Barnyard Muck.

THE PART WHERE MOM MAKES POPCORN

Scoot over," Mom said, plopping down on the couch next to me Sunday night. I made room. She'd brought popcorn, after all.

"Here," Mom said, handing me my own bowl. "Extra butter."

Mom and I watched a rerun of a chef show and ate without talking. Mom gets like that—quiet, I mean—when she's had a hard day in the ER. Especially when she's had to treat little kids.

"How was school?" Mom asked during a commercial.

I shrugged.

"Everything going okay with the play?" I wasn't sure how to answer that.

"Dad said that you seemed a little down after rehearsal on Friday," Mom admitted.

"Someone was being kind of mean is all," I said.

"Is someone bullying you?"

I shook my head. "No. It's not like that exactly." I told her what happened when we painted the barn. How Paige said, in front of everyone, that I shouldn't say Monica's line because I'd mess her up. And how Annie defended her.

Mom raised her eyebrows. "Ah. Got it." She wrapped her arm around my shoulder and was quiet for a minute. "Putting together a play takes a lot of work. Everybody is bound to get stressed out now and then."

"So you're saying I *should* cut Paige some slack?" I asked her.

"I don't know about Paige; I was talking about Annie," Mom said.

What did Annie have to be stressed out about? Thanks to Paige, she had the perfect wig for her costume. And she was getting acting tips from someone who'd been in a commercial.

"Can we just go back to watching TV?" I asked.

"Sure," Mom said. "But I'm here if you ever want to talk."

I sighed.

"Sorry," Mom said, nudging me. "I have to say things like that. It's in the Mom Handbook."

"What does the handbook say about making more popcorn?" I teased her.

"It says if you want more, you have to help."

I followed her to the kitchen. Mom made popcorn on the stovetop with a covered pot and hot oil. She said she liked the *ping ping* the kernels made when they popped. She offered to make it that way when I have a sleepover. But the way things were going with Annie, I wondered if that would ever happen.

BALL OF FIRE

We were practicing our *danjun* breathing at taekwondo. Your *danjun* is the space right below your belly button. It's not an actual body part, but it's where your life energy, or *ki*, is stored, according to Master Kim and other people. It felt weird to be standing with my eyes closed. Usually the only time we closed our eyes in class was when we sat in meditation. Closing your eyes any other time could get you accidentally wonked on the nose by your training partner.

"Inhale deeply," Master Kim told the class. We were supposed to fill our lungs all the way to the bottom.

"Rest your hand on your midsection," Master Kim

instructed. "If you are doing this correctly, you should feel your stomach push out a little."

Master Kim explained that most people only used the top part of their lungs most of the time. He said not to worry if we were having a hard time, we'd get better with practice. I found it easy, though. We did a deep breathing exercise to warm up before rehearsals. Mrs. Delany, like Master Kim, believed controlling your breathing was an important skill to have. Your brain and body worked better when they had more oxygen.

After a while, Master Kim said we could open our eyes. We were going to add visualization and movement. I liked visualization. It was a good way to practice stuff without really practicing. Sometimes, when I couldn't fall asleep at night, I visualized doing my form or saying my lines onstage.

Master Kim went on. "This time, when you inhale, bring your hands up as if you are holding a small ball in front of your chest," he said, demonstrating. "Next, slowly push the ball out in front of you as you exhale."

It was easy enough to imagine holding a ball. (Maybe because we did that kind of stuff when we improv-ed at rehearsal, too.) But then it got a little strange. Master Kim told us to think of the imaginary ball as a red, glowing ball of fire.

"Imagine the ball is your power and it is traveling from your *danjun* and then through your arms and finally out your hands," he said.

Another yellow belt raised his hand. "Is it like using the Force in *Star Wars?*" he asked.

Master Kim smiled. "If it helps you to think of it that way, yes."

We spent a few minutes picking up and extending our "balls of fire" out in front of us in slow motion. Inhaaale. Exhaaale. And then we moved on to punching. We did that in slow motion, too.

"Imagine all your power concentrated in one, tiny spot as you connect with your target," Master Kim said.

I didn't understand how punching slowly in the air would help me break my board. All I knew was that my gold-belt test was in less than three weeks and I wasn't sure if I had a fire in my belly or a swarm of butterflies.

SCHEDULING CONFLICTS, PART 2

On Tuesday morning Annie told me Mo-mo had to take her car to the mechanic.

"That means she'll have to drive the Red Rabbit," Annie said. The Red Rabbit was what her family called their sports car. It had only two seats.

"I hope that doesn't mean you'll have to miss rehearsal," she said. "Sorry!"

I told Dad at dinner. "I need a ride home from rehearsal on Thursday. Can you do it this one time?"

"I thought you rode with Annie."

"She can't do it Thursday."

"I'm sorry, kiddo. I can't," Dad said as he set the table for dinner (mac-and-cheese from a box).

"But I can't miss. The play is in four weeks and Mrs. Delany says every rehearsal counts."

"It's not like you have a bunch of lines," Sam said.

I scowled at my brother at the same time Dad said, "Watch it!"

"What? I'm only trying to help," Sam said.

Dad turned back to me. "Could you ride with someone else? Another cast member?"

"Yeah," Sam said. "What about that boy? Your boyfriend JJ?"

Dad shot him another warning look.

"If you can't find another ride, you'll just have to ride the bus home and miss rehearsal," Dad told me. "It's only one day. I'm sure the director will understand."

"But . . ."

"You'll figure this out. I have faith in you."

BETWEEN A ROCK
AND A MEGAN PLACE

Later on, Sam strolled into my room while I was finishing up the homework I didn't get to while I was at rehearsal.

"Hey E. I have to stay after marching band on Thursday for a drum-line meeting," he said. "But I talked to Megan and she said she can give you a ride. If you want."

My brain paced back and forth.

Sam rocked back on his heels. "Well? Usually how it works is when someone says something, you respond."

"I . . ."

"You like Megan, right?"

"Yeah," I lied. "She's nice." (*When she's not taking all your attention or showing up for dinner and making me miss taekwondo.*)

"Okay then." He grinned. "I'll tell her it's a go."

Swell bells.

BANANA-MOBILE

Sam was right. Megan's car was impossible to miss. It was yellow.

"Hiya, Eliza!" she said when I climbed in. "I wasn't sure which door you'd be coming out of. I'm glad I got it right. I was thinking the front door but then I saw all the cars going this way to the side door. Figured I'd take a chance." She was rambling, like I did when I got nervous.

The inside of her car was spotless. It smelled nice, too. And there was one of those cardboard air fresheners hanging from the mirror. It was shaped like a banana.

"Buckle up!" she said, even though I always did.

Ten minutes. That's all I had to survive and then I'd be home.

"So, how was rehearsal?" Megan asked.

"It was good." And then, because I was nervous, too, my mouth started running like it was in a race.

"Today was Shoe Day," I said. "That means we all got to start wearing the shoes we're going to wear for the show so we can get used to moving around in them. My friend Annie got to wear these kitten slippers we found at Goodwill. I'm one of the Three Little Pigs, so we're just wearing tennis shoes."

Megan kept her eyes on the road and smiled. "Sounds like fun. Did Sam tell you that we might play in the pit for the spring musical?"

"What's that?" I asked her.

"The pit crew? Oh! Well, at the high school, the stage has a lowered part in front. People sit down in it to play the music for a show."

I bet Annie knew that. It was probably in the theater book. I could drag my copy out from under the bed, but if I started carrying it around and reading it, Mom might wonder where it'd been all this time.

"I played in the pit last year as a freshman," Megan said. "It was a *ton* of fun."

Great. If Sam played for the spring musical, I'd never see him next semester, either.

"The pit was all I could handle," Megan said. "I could never actually be onstage like you. That's so brave."

I couldn't tell if she was being nice or really meant it. But Master Kim said there were three things you should accept graciously: victories, defeats, and compliments.

"So," Megan said. (She sure said "so" a lot.) "Any cute guys in the cast or crew? Or girls?" she added quickly.

I didn't want to talk to her about that, but my brain forgot to tell my mouth.

"There's this guy named JJ. But I'm not sure what the deal is."

Instead of teasing me, like Sam would have, or launching into some big life lecture like Mom or Dad would have, Megan nodded thoughtfully. "Yeah. It can be confusing. Do you like him?"

"Maybe. I'm not sure," I said.

"Does he like you?"

"I don't know."

"Well, in my experience, guys usually give you a sign."

"What kind of sign?" I wondered.

She shrugged. "It depends on the guy. You usually just know when you see it, though."

I was supposed to wait for some kind of random sign? I wished there was a book like Annie's theater book about this stuff.

I leaned back in the seat, suddenly tired from rehearsal. Megan turned up the speakers. "Ooo! This is my favorite song!"

Megan hit REPLAY and we listened to her favorite song two more times before pulling into my driveway. I was okay with that. It meant I didn't have to think of more things to say.

"Thanks for the ride," I said, unbuckling my seat belt.

"No problem!" Megan said. "And hey, I'm looking forward to going to the opening night of your play in two weeks."

Toothpicks! Sam had invited Megan to come to the play. I knew I shouldn't be surprised. He said he was going to. Did that mean she was coming to dinner with us, too? That was supposed to be a family—

Wait. What?

"Three weeks," I told her.

She looked confused.

"The play is three weeks from tomorrow."

Megan looked like she just found out she forgot to study for a big test. "Oh no," she said. "That's the night of the Fall Semiformal!"

NOTE TO SELF: MOM SAYING "HONEY" IS A BAD SIGN

Mom checked the calendar and sighed. "I guess Sam told me the wrong date before. I'm sorry, Eliza."

"But he's coming to the play, right?" I asked her.

"Honey . . ." Any sentence that started that way usually wasn't good.

"He said he would!" I reminded her.

"I know," Mom said. "But you have to understand. The dance is important."

"My play is more important." *And I planned for everyone to go to dinner beforehand and be together and have a fun family night like we used to!*

"I know it's important, but the dance is important to your brother, too. He's made plans. What do you want me to do?"

My eyes stung with tears but I blinked them back. "You said you'd make him go, remember? You said you'd drag Dad and Sam there 'kicking and screaming.'"

Mom reached out to rub my shoulder. "Eliza. Making Sam go to your play and miss the dance would affect other people."

"You mean Megan," I said.

Mom nodded. "Yes. I mean Megan."

I scowled.

"Dad and I will be there," Mom said. I gave her the stink eye.

"Look. You can ask him to go to the play instead," Mom said. "But I wouldn't get your hopes up." Pause. "And I won't make him."

That was it. My plan for getting my family together for opening night was dead, dead, dead.

CRANKY PANTS

One time, when Bear was about a year old, Dad decided it would be a great idea if he took her for a run. So he climbed on his bike, attached a long leash to Bear's collar, and headed out. The plan was to go to the railroad tracks on the outskirts of our neighborhood and loop back. Only once they got there, Bear sat down and refused to move. Dad ended up having to carry her home in one arm while he pushed his bike with the other.

We were all Bear at the end of Friday's rehearsal.

It wasn't just because Mrs. Delany had extended rehearsals by an hour. Things had gone haywire from the beginning when someone forgot to bring snacks and Cole ran to the teachers' lounge to snag some pretzel rods. A couple of kids started using them like swords, which made a mess, and Mrs. Delany gave a lecture about respecting our theater space.

Then once we got down to work, it seemed as if everyone had suddenly forgotten their lines or their blocking. And finally, right in the middle of things, the light board died and it took the tech crew twenty minutes to figure out how to bring the stage lights back up.

"All right, friends," Mrs. Delany said. "It seems as if we've worn our cranky pants today, so let's just try to end on a productive note."

We gathered in an arc on the stage. I followed Annie even though she sat down near Paige and her posse. Maybe Mom had been right about cutting Annie some slack.

"All right," Mrs. Delany said. "I have some notes before we go for the day." Everyone pulled out their scripts and pencils.

Melted peppermint ice cream! "I forgot my script," I whispered to Annie. "I left it in my locker."

Paige glared at me. "Shhhh."

"Can I share yours?" I asked Annie. She looked nervous but nudged her script a few inches my direction.

Paige raised her hand. "Mrs. Delany. Eliza doesn't have her script."

DIABOLICAL DIRECTOR

Mrs. Delany gave a tired smile, which made me feel even worse about forgetting. "Friends, what are rules number 3 through 5 for scripts?" she asked.

The group recited it together: "Always bring it to rehearsal."

Mrs. Delany turned to me. "Looks like we get to experience another round of Diabolical Director!"

The rest of the group let out a small cheer. But all I could think was *Oh no*.

We'd played Diabolical Director when two other people had forgotten to bring their scripts. The rules went like this: the person who forgot their script stood in the middle of the circle, while each person took turns giving them a direction. The hard part was that you didn't just do one thing; each direction got added to the previous ones. So by the time you made it around the whole circle, you had to memorize a couple dozen directions!

"You know the drill," Mrs. Delany said to me. "Eliza Bing, do you accept the challenge that's been placed before you?"

Even though she was asking, I knew there was no getting out of it. No one ever backed out of Diabolical Director, because it would show you weren't a team player. And being a team player was, like, Rule 1 in theater.

Plus, I had to admit, it looked like a *little* fun to be in the middle. I agreed.

"All right! Everybody on your feet. Make a circle and make it snappy," called Mrs. Delany.

In no time flat, I was surrounded. Mrs. Delany picked JJ to start things off.

"You are out for a stroll in the park," he said. I began walking around the middle of the circle.

Vivian and Kate were next. "It's a sunny day," Kate said. I put my hand up to shield my eyes.

"It's hot."

I fanned myself with my other hand and kept walking.

The rest of the people in the circle weren't quite as easy. Pretty soon, there was a marching band to dodge and someone handed me a kite to fly and then I noticed I was late, so I had to keep checking my fake watch every once in a while.

I did my best to keep up but it was like being a bouncy ball loose on the playground. When I forgot something, though, there was always someone to remind me.

"Don't forget to hum the 'Alphabet Song'!"

"Where's your umbrella?" (Yep. It started "raining.")

People laughed. But it was okay—I was laughing at myself, too. I was right; being in the middle was fun.

Well, it was until it was Annie's turn to give me a direction. "Oh no! Watch out. You just stepped on a giant beehive!"

I couldn't believe she said that! Annie *knew* I was afraid of bees. And now I had to hop around, pretending to get stung.

Monica took it from there. Her direction was "The bees

are everywhere!" So I started swatting and hopping and dodging marching-band people and checking my watch and humming.

Paige was last. "And now you're having an allergic reaction."

Some people were laughing so hard they were rolled over, holding their sides.

How was I supposed to follow that direction? I started scratching like crazy.

"Aaannnd, that's a wrap!" Mrs. Delany called. She shook my hand. "Thanks for being a good sport, Eliza. And please don't forget your script again."

BEST FRIEND . . . ?

Are you mad about the bees?" Annie asked after rehearsal. I didn't say anything.

"They weren't real, you know," she teased.

"Why did you pick something I'm afraid of?" I demanded.

"Paige says acting is about being vulnerable," Annie said. "Plus, I thought it would be easy."

"It wasn't. It was hard," I said.

"It wasn't that hard," she argued. "Besides, you did a great job. You always do." She said this last part like she was annoyed.

We stared at each other. I had so many things I wanted to say. But this is what I blurted out: "Why are you still hanging out with her?"

"Who? Paige?"

"Yes. Paige. You said you were hanging out with her so you could get some tips," I said, my voice shaking. "Don't you have enough already?"

Annie shrugged. "She's nice." I made a face. "She *is*! You don't know her like I do."

I bit my bottom lip to keep it from trembling.

Annie stood up straighter. "Eliza. Don't be jealous. *You're* my best friend."

It was the first time Annie had called me her best friend. Too bad it didn't feel like it.

BULL'S-EYE

To celebrate me getting my yellow belt over the summer, Mom had given me fifty dollars. She thought I'd buy a cake-decorating kit, but instead I bought a used kicking bag that Dad found for sale on a bulletin board on campus. There was tons of duct tape all over it, but it worked great when I wanted to practice kicks or punches. It definitely didn't work for practicing hammer fists. I learned this the hard way the first time I hit the top and discovered there was a piece of hard plastic there. That's why I was practicing for my board break on a throw pillow when Sam walked by my room Saturday afternoon.

"Yo, E. What'd your bed ever do to you?" he asked.

I ignored him and hit the pillow again. *"Huuup!"*

When he didn't go away, I said, "My gold-belt test is in two weeks."

"Oh yeah?"

"You wanna come watch?" I asked him. He hadn't come to my first test, but I thought it was worth a shot.

"Can't," he said. "The marching band is in a Veterans Day parade that day."

I hit the pillow a few more times. This time with more force. *"Huuup! Huuup! Huuup!"*

Sam kept standing there, watching. Which made me angrier.

"Why are you so mad?" he asked. "It's not like I scheduled the band thing, you know."

I stopped throwing hammer fists. "No. But your stupid band thing means Mom will miss it, too."

"Hey! Band isn't stupid."

I started breathing hard. It was bad enough Sam wasn't coming to the show and now Mom wasn't going to come to my gold-belt test, either. And why hadn't anyone bothered to tell me this before now? It was like I was an afterthought in my own family.

"Why does Mom always have to do *your* thing?" I said.

"She's the band nurse, idiot."

When Sam saw my face, he said, "Come on. You know I didn't mean it."

I did. But I went back to punching and concentrated on putting all my power into my fist anyway. It was better than crying in front of my brother.

"You're being impossible," Sam said.

"Go away. I'm busy."

"Fine," he said. But he didn't leave. "Is there something I can do to help you get ready, at least?"

"You could let me hit *you*," I said. He knew I really wouldn't hit him. Not only was he a foot taller, but taekwondo was about avoiding fights, not starting them.

Sam abruptly left. But he came back a few minutes later, carrying a roll of the red tape he used to tape up his drumsticks. "Move," he said, bumping his hip into mine.

As I watched, he used the tape to make a bull's-eye on the pillow. "Here," he said, stepping back. "Now you have a better target."

I was still mad.

MORE BAD NEWS

On Sunday night, Mom sat at the kitchen table and studied the revised schedule Mrs. Delany sent home.

"Rehearsals are an hour longer," I told her. Mrs. D had stressed how important it was to point that out to our parents.

"Ooo. That'll work out great!" Mom said.

"It will?"

"Yeah. Starting next week, Dad should be able to pick you up."

"But I ride with Annie." (I was still mad at her about the bee thing, but how were we going to make up if we didn't get to hang out by ourselves?)

"Well, now we don't have to be a burden," Mom said.

I wasn't a burden. At least I didn't think I was.

TRICKS AND TREATS

Tuesday was Halloween, so Mrs. Delany wore a yellow cowboy hat during rehearsal. Well, at least for part of rehearsal. She kept changing hats throughout the afternoon. At some point she had on: a top hat, a jester's hat, a beanie with a propeller, and a knitted hat with a long yarn braid that was supposed to look like Rapunzel's hair.

"Halloween is my favorite holiday!" she told us as she passed out fake vampire teeth at the end of the day. She made everyone line up and say "Trick or treat," and then demanded a trick.

"Come on, friends! You have to think on your feet onstage," she said.

Vivian told a joke. JJ did a handstand. Annie recited the alphabet backwards. For my trick, I whistled. I should have counted to ten in Korean instead, but I didn't think of it until afterwards.

I showed Mom the teeth when I got home. She loved them. "You should wear them while we hand out candy," she said. "Dad's on Bear duty this year." Bear went nuts when she saw costumes so someone had to hang out with her upstairs.

Mom brought out a blanket for us to sit on since our cement porch was chilly. (I skipped the vampire teeth; they made talking hard.) It felt strange handing out candy instead of collecting it. But I didn't have anyone to go out with. Sam was off with his friends. I thought Annie might invite me over to her neighborhood—where it was a really big deal, practically a block party—but she didn't. Which didn't make any sense to me since she'd said I was her best friend just last week. Maybe she'd decided not to go this year.

Mom and I had been camped outside for about twenty minutes when Mrs. Kelly showed up carrying her two-year-old while her four-year-old ran ahead. The Kellys lived a few houses up the street from us.

"Trick or treat!" Chris, the four-year-old, said as he arrived at our step. His brother was dressed like a pumpkin. But instead of saying "Trick or treat," he wailed and tightened his grip around Mrs. Kelly's neck and hip.

Mom commented on Chris's firefighter costume, thanked him for protecting the neighborhood, and put a couple of mini candy bars into his pail.

"Eliza," Mrs. Kelly said. "I'm glad you're home! I need a favor. The baby is having a meltdown. Would you want to take Chris around for a bit so he can get his candy? It would be such a huge help for me."

"Of course," I told her. "I'd love to."

"Oh, thank you!" Mrs. Kelly knelt down and asked Chris if it'd be okay if I took him trick-or-treating.

Chris nodded and then looked at me. "But where's your costume?" I ran inside and grabbed my apron, a wooden spoon, and a plastic mixing bowl. It wasn't fancy, but I thought it was a pretty decent Sweet Caroline for a few minutes' notice.

I took Chris's hand and the two of us made our way down the block and back on the other side. Even though I didn't say "Trick or treat," a lot of the houses put candy in my bowl, too. When he was ready, I walked Chris back to his own house. He giggled when he rang his own doorbell.

"Thank you again, Eliza," Mrs. Kelly said after Chris ran inside. "You're a real lifesaver!"

I'd been called lots of things before. Spaz. Every Day Eliza. Quitter. Nimbus. Lifesaver felt so much better.

A GOOD MARTIAL ARTIST (NOT)

The week before my first belt test, Madison had warned me classes got more crowded closer to Test Day. She was right.

Master Kim and Miss Abigail were busy with two groups, so the rest of us were supposed to be working on our *poomsae*, or forms, on our own.

I ran through *kicho ee bo* a couple of times. Since I had messed it up in class and prompted Master Kim to give his "A good martial artist shows confidence at all times" talk, I'd been practicing. I did *not* want to mess up at the test. I'd gotten so confident that I could do the form facing any direction. I could even do it facing a corner. Miss Abigail once told a group of us that she'd seen Master Kim make black-belt students do their forms wearing blindfolds. But she might have been teasing.

I took a break. "Eliza?" Sophia asked. "Can you please help me with my form?"

"Sure," I told her. The two of us walked to an open spot on the carpet.

"I can do the first part," Sophia said. "But I can't remember what comes in the middle."

"Let's do it together," I said. "It's always easier for me when I watch someone else. I'll go slow."

I stood a few feet in front of Sophia so she could watch me, and we went through her form. We were doing the last part when Master Kim came over. I *kihap*ed extra loud. It always felt good to get his attention. Master Kim almost never gave out compliments.

"Those last punches should be to the torso, not the face," Master Kim said.

Sophia lowered her punch in the air. I did, too. My cheeks burned.

"Sorry," I muttered to Sophia after we'd returned to ready position.

Master Kim looked at me. "It was a mistake, Eliza. A good martial artist knows that a misstep is not something to be ashamed of but a chance to change direction."

"Yes, sir," I said, and bowed.

"White belts, please make a line," Master Kim called.

Sophia and the rest of the white belts joined him to go over their form together.

I hightailed it to the side of the room to join the yellow and gold belts to wait for our turn.

"What'd'ya get that for?" a boy next to me asked, pointing at my Spirit Award patch. He was new and looked around seven. "It's neat."

I tried to ignore him. We weren't supposed to be talking while we waited. The boy poked me. "How do you get one?"

I turned and raised my finger to my lips. His mouth made an *Oh* and then he nodded.

My cheeks were still warm about steering Sophia in the wrong direction. I hoped I didn't confuse her too much. I also hoped Master Kim didn't ask people to give their special patches back.

THE ~~SECOND-TO~~-LAST RIDE WITH ANNIE

Annie and I were in the backseat of her mom's car, going over my taekwondo flash cards. I was still trying to forget about the whole bee thing. Best friends forgive each other, right? Besides, Annie had chosen to hang out with me at the last two rehearsals.

"How do you say 'hammer fist'?" Annie asked.

"*Mejoomuk.*"

"Right!"

"Well, it's my board break," I told her, and laughed. "I better know it."

"You know what? I should come watch a class sometime," Annie said. "Or try it out. If I'm going to be an actor, it might come in handy someday to know how to fight."

The thought of Annie coming to a taekwondo class was exciting. But I was glad she didn't suggest coming to watch my test. Tests were already nerve-wracking.

"Yeah," I told her. "You could be an action hero."

"I'd need a stage name, though," she said. "Annie Young-Mays doesn't sound very tough."

I agreed with her, but her mom fake-complained from the front seat. "You're awfully cheeky for a girl who needs my permission to get her ears double-pierced," Mo-mo said.

"You're getting your ears pierced again?" I asked. "When?"

Annie chewed the edge of her thumb. "Um. Tomorrow. After rehearsal."

"That's cool," I told her. "I've wanted to get my ears pierced since forever. I beg my mom every birthday and Christmas, but she worries about them getting infected."

"I'd invite you, but Paige's mom is driving," Annie said. "And I don't think there's enough room since a few other people from the cast are going, too. The moms are meeting us there to sign the forms and then going out for coffee."

I suddenly felt bad for me *and* Mom. We were both getting left out.

"It's okay," I told Annie, turning away from her a bit. "My mom has to work anyway. Things are always super crazy at the ER on Fridays."

Annie looked relieved. "Thanks for understanding."

Mo-mo glanced in the rearview mirror. "Annie was supposed to tell you that we won't be able to give you a ride home," she said to me. "Did she let you know?"

I shook my head. Apparently there were a couple of things Annie didn't tell me.

FEARLESSNESS

Why so glum, chum?" Dad asked me after dinner. He and Mom were doing the dishes. They did that sometimes, even though we had a dishwasher. They called it a married couple's date. (Mom washed, Dad dried.)

I told him about Annie not being able to give me a ride the next day, though I didn't tell him why. "I guess I'll just have to miss rehearsal and ride the bus."

"Tell you what," Dad said. "How about I play hooky from my last class? That way you can go to rehearsal, and I'll pick you up."

Mom frowned at him.

"Just this once," he promised her. Then he turned back to me. "Besides, I could use a mental-health day."

Even though there wasn't any bubble gum around to whack me in the head like there was in the store when I hatched my plan to become the best best friend, I got another idea.

The next night, I put it into motion.

"So what would you like for dinner?" Dad asked when he picked me up. "It's just the two of us. Mom and Sam have an away game." He gave me the perfect opening.

"How 'bout the food court?"

"At the mall?"

I nodded.

Dad considered it. "Okay. Why not? But don't tell

Mom. She thinks we eat baked chicken and salads when she's gone."

I laughed.

When we pulled into the parking lot, I convinced Dad to park on the side farthest from the food court. "At least we can get some exercise walking in," I said.

I had no idea when Annie, Paige, and whoever else was getting their ears pierced were planning to be there. But we had to walk past the jewelry store in order to get to the food court.

I had the whole story worked out. Dad and I just happened to be at the mall. (He needed a new dress shirt.) And I just happened to have brought enough money. The only tricky part was going to be convincing Dad to sign the permission form. At least he was usually easier to persuade than Mom.

My heart pounded as we got closer to the jewelry store. As casually as I could, I looked inside. They do the piercings right in front of the window.

But no one was there. Except a little boy trying to climb into the chair.

Bummer.

Dad and I made it to the food court. He grabbed a sub and I stood in line for chicken strips. He spent the first part of dinner telling me about a project he was doing at school. That was okay with me because I felt like sitting and listening and not thinking about how disappointed I was that I'd missed Annie. Getting our ears pierced together would have been the perfect best best friend activity. I guess it was a crazy plan to begin with.

Eventually Dad finished talking about his class, and he asked about the play. "It seems like you're enjoying it," he said.

"I am," I told him. "I really like Mrs. Delany, the director, too."

I told him about some of the games and improv exercises we played and how we were still working on blocking. Which Mrs. D called "controlled chaos."

"What's your favorite part of being in the play?"

I considered this. "Probably improv. No rules," I explained.

"What's your least favorite part?" Dad asked.

"When it's over."

Dad laughed. "I always thought you belonged onstage," he said.

"You did?"

Dad seemed surprised. "Of course! You've just got this thing about you. A fearlessness."

The compliment made me smile. I didn't know about fearless. I had plenty of fears. Like I was losing my best friend, for one.

NOT TODAY

When Dad and I walked past the jewelry store on our way out, Annie was there!

Her eyes grew three sizes when I walked in. "Eliza! What are you doing here?" she said. I couldn't tell if she was happy or just shocked to see me.

"Uh. My dad and I were having dinner," I said.

"Hi, Mr. Bing," Annie said.

Dad swept his gaze around the half circle of girls. "Good evening, young ladies," Dad replied. Ugh. He sounded like such a dork.

Paige was there. So were Monica and a girl named Stephanie. They all waved politely to my dad before he wandered over to where the moms were. (He'd probably call them young ladies, too.)

"What are you doing?" I asked Annie, although I could clearly see they were picking out the earrings they wanted.

"I think we should go with this one," Paige said, ignoring me and pointing to a fake diamond stud on the sample board.

Annie turned to me. "Since you're here, I need your opinion."

Yes! She wanted my opinion. "I like the blue one," I told her.

"Hmmm. I'm not sure. . . ."

"Maybe I'll get it," I said.

"You're getting your ears pierced, too?" Annie asked.

"Sure. Why not?"

Annie smiled. "Sweet!"

My secret mission was working out perfectly! I could finally get my ears pierced and Annie and I would be able to do it together. I wondered if we'd hold each other's hands. Best friends did that kind of thing when they were nervous.

Dad and the other parents followed the jewelry-store employee over to piercing area. She was going over the permission forms. She paused. "I'm sorry. Did I miss you?" she said to Dad. "Do you need a form, too?"

Dad laughed. "No. I definitely don't need a form. Thanks."

Paige snickered. I ignored her and stepped closer. "Can I, Dad?" I pleaded.

He shook his head. "Nope. Your mother would kill me." Some of the moms chuckled.

"Please?" I asked. I stared him down, giving my best puppy-dog eyes. You could usually get Dad to break with logic, so I tried that, too. "I'm old enough to take care of them," I said.

The seconds and silence stretched over the whole store. But Dad stood firm. "Not today."

There was more snickering behind me.

Dad's phone buzzed. "Excuse me, gotta take this," he told everyone, and then said he'd meet me outside.

Annie stepped over. "Maybe you should just go, too," she whispered.

I turned so fast I probably gave myself whiplash. "You want me to leave?"

"N-no," Annie stammered. "It's just that, well . . ."

"I'm embarrassing you."

"I didn't say that. I'm just with my other friends," she said. "We'll do something else together soon. I promise."

"So who's first?" the girl with the piercing gun asked.

"Me," Paige said.

The girls went back to filling out forms and talking about which earrings they were going to get. "Are you going to stay and watch?" the saleslady asked me.

I shook my head. No. All I wanted to do was leave before I started blubbering like a baby.

Right before I stepped out, I heard Paige mutter, "Aaaawkward."

And then I heard everyone laugh. I wasn't a hundred percent, but I was pretty sure Annie laughed, too.

WHAT ANNIE TEXTED ME LATER THAT NIGHT

I'm sorry you couldn't stay

A GOOD MARTIAL ARTIST KNOWS WHEN TO CHANGE DIRECTION

If I had the Rules to Surviving Sixth Grade notebook, I would have added No. 37: Never get pizza on a rainy day. The soggy square on my tray went perfectly with my Monday morning.

Annie wasn't in homeroom, so I didn't get a chance to talk to her about what happened at the jewelry store. Not that I knew what I was going to say anyway.

I sat down at our usual table and waited. I'd seen her come into the lunchroom while I was in line, but there'd been no sign of her since.

Maybe I'd practice my taekwondo memorization. I'd

just started going through my backpack for my flash cards when Annie arrived and put her tray down across from me. "Why didn't you text me back?" she asked.

I was hurt. I was mad. I was embarrassed.

"I figured you were busy," I said.

"I was, but not too busy for you."

"Could've fooled me."

Annie raised an eyebrow. "You're being kinda rude again," she said.

"Am I?"

"Yes. You are. Look, I'm really sorry I couldn't invite you. I wasn't the one who planned it."

"But you went along," I said. "And then you laughed when Paige said 'Aaawkward.'"

Annie's eyes widened. "No I didn't!"

"You didn't?"

"No," she said, crossing her arms over her chest. "I would never do something like that!"

The two of us stared at each other for a minute.

I hate this. Best friends aren't supposed to fight.

"I'm sorry," I told her.

Annie dropped her arms. "Me too," she said. "Can we start over?"

I said, "Sure." So she got up, took her tray, and walked around a nearby table. Then she sat back down across from me. "Hey!" she said, all cheerful.

"Hey," I said, playing along.

Annie asked me if anything was new and I told her

about taekwondo class. I left out the part about messing Sophia up, though.

"What's new with you?" I asked her.

Annie paused. "Well," she said, "I got some new earrings."

"Cool," I said, so she'd know it was okay to talk about them.

Annie grinned. "What do you think?" she asked, pulling back her hair so I could see.

They were the earrings Paige picked out.

KNOCK, KNOCK. WHO'S THERE? MORE TROUBLE AT REHEARSAL

There are ten days till opening night, friends!" Mrs. Delany called. "We're in the home stretch!"

Mrs. Delany didn't need to remind us. Everyone was stressed out. Big-time. People were still tripping over lines. Or over pieces of sets that were in the wrong place—or over crew members touching up paint. And the light and sound people hadn't gotten all the cues down. To top it off, everyone was super tired from the long rehearsals. It was like the closer we got, the harder it seemed to find the energy. Even Mrs. Delany had circles under her eyes and sounded hoarse.

"All righty," our director said. "Today's goal is to get a full run-through."

A "run-through" meant what it sounded like: going through the whole play without stopping. Or with as little stopping as possible. It was tricky because the tech crew was still working on making the scene changes smoothly. Sometimes they forgot to bring out part of the set.

Or dropped a prop.

Clank!

"Sorry!" a stage ninja named Mary said. She picked up the fire poker. (Stage "ninjas" got their nicknames because, during the play, they wore all black.)

Paige sighed dramatically. She'd been doing that a lot. "There are too many distractions. How am I supposed to concentrate?" she asked.

Mary apologized a second time and hurried off. I wondered quietly out loud how Paige would react if someone's phone rang or they started snoring in the middle of the actual play.

"She'd probably stop the play and scold them," Vivian said.

"And then make everyone start over," JJ added.

The three of us giggled.

JJ, Vivian, and I played a bunch of rounds of War in the wings and stayed out of the way until it was our turn to be onstage. The three of us were part of a group of fairy-tale and nursery-rhyme characters that included Jack and Jill Hill, Jack Beanstalk (who got to carry kidney beans spray-painted gold), the Pooped Piper (who got to act sleepy the whole time!), and Humpty Grumpty (an extra-cranky version of the famous egg). For the actual performance, we'd have to hang out backstage or in the hallway and wait for Cole to come tell us when to go on. Annie had to hang out with the people from her act.

I was down to a stack of twelve cards when it was *finally* time to go onstage.

In our scene, the fairy-tale characters were milling around, just doing their daily business. Fetching water, fluffing a pillow for a nap, stuff like that. Vivian, JJ, and I were pretending to chat with a street vendor selling sticks. The script called for Cinder Ellen (Paige) to come bursting through the door of a shop and start talking about the Barnyard Bash and how she'd hoped she'd get an invitation.

Rob, the boy playing the farmer's son, strolled across the stage. "Hot diggity! The e-vites go out today!" he called.

That was Paige's cue line. Only the set door was stuck. She rattled the handle a few times. But nothing.

"Oh for Pete's sake," Paige cried, knocking on the door. "Someone let me out!"

My mouth worked faster than my brain again. "Not by the hair of my snouty snout snout!" I answered.

The entire stage erupted in laughter. I soaked it in and bobbed on my toes like the stage was a bouncy house.

"Hold!" Mrs. Delany called. One of the stage ninjas rushed onstage to open the door for Paige from the outside.

"Eliza, that was brilliant!" Mrs. Delany said. "I think we should add it to the scene."

From the doorway of the now-open door, Paige crossed her arms and set her jaw.

"Paige, make the change in your script," Mrs. Delany said. "You too, Eliza."

"But Mrs. D," Paige said, "don't you think it messes up the flow of the scene?"

Mrs. Delany shook her head. "The audience will eat it up. I wish *I* had thought of it," she said, and gave me a wink. "It's my all-time favorite ad-lib."

Paige tried a different approach. "But isn't it too late to make changes? The show is next week."

"It's never too late for great," Mrs. Delany said.

THE PART WHERE PAIGE STOPPED ME AFTER REHEARSAL

On my way to the parking lot, Paige grabbed my elbow and pulled me aside.

"Tell Mrs. Delany you don't want to do the new line," she said.

"Why?"

"Because it messes things up!"

"Mrs. Delany doesn't think so."

I could tell she wanted to say something bad about Mrs. Delany but decided against it.

"Look," she said, poking my shoulder. "This may be your first school play, but this is super important to me. The high school drama director is coming to watch. And I want to make a good impression so next year I can be the first freshman to land a lead."

"That's a good goal," I told her. Because it actually was.

She looked surprised. "Thanks. So you'll talk to Mrs. Delany about the line, then?"

I shrugged.

"Please? I'll owe you one. What do you want?"

Stop trying to steal my best friend.

"I'm sorry," I said.

Then she called me a bad name and walked away.

ANNIE

Dad was running late. Mo-mo didn't want me waiting by myself, so Annie and I sat on the curb.

"Isn't it cool about the new line?" I asked.

Annie hugged her knees and didn't say anything.

"Don't you like it?" I said.

"It's funny."

"You don't seem very excited."

"I said it was funny."

"Well, that's a good thing, right?" I said.

Annie turned her head my direction. "My book says a production is more important than any one person."

I was confused. Was she trying to tell me that I wasn't important?

A car turned into the parking lot. Annie and I looked, but it wasn't Dad.

"Paige said she thinks I should get Mrs. Delany to change her mind," I said.

Annie made a noise that sounded like *hmmmm*.

"What do you think?" I asked.

"I dunno," she answered. "I guess you should do what you want."

I thought about this. "I like the line. Mrs. Delany says it'll get a big laugh. I wanna do it."

"Of course you do."

"What's that supposed to mean?" I asked.

"Nothing," she said.

Only it was the kind of *nothing* that was *something*. I was trying to figure out a way to ask her why she was so cranky when Dad pulled in. I stood up.

"Thanks for waiting with me," I told her. She took my outstretched hand and let me her haul up.

I headed toward my car at the same time Annie headed back to hers. The two of us bumped into each other and then did that weird thing people sometimes do when they're trying to work out how to get around each other.

After a few seconds of back and forth, I said, "Dear sir, I regret I cannot dance. My boots are killing me."

Annie was supposed to say the next line from the play ("I'll forgive you this once, ma'am"), but instead she waited for me to pick a direction.

"See ya," she said as she got in her car.

I'd been right that time we practiced arm bars in tae-kwondo: it was definitely surprising how fast things could go from okay to not okay.

TEST DAY

At my yellow-belt test, I didn't know what to expect. At least this time I didn't freak out when I saw the long table at the front of the room with the fancy covering and the three judges' chairs.

Sophia, the white belt I'd been helping, stood at the edge of the room. "Don't be nervous," I told her. "Be awesome!"

That's what Madison had told me at our last test. And right before the play auditions. I saw her yesterday in the hall and she wished me luck. She was finally off crutches for her bum knee, but still didn't know when she'd get to go back to her taekwondo class.

I showed Sophia where to sign in and then said, "We should warm up." We joined the rest of the students who were stretching and running through their forms one last time.

At precisely one o'clock, Master Kim and two other black belts walked into the room and stood behind the table. I knew from testing before that one of the judges was Master Kim's brother. I didn't recognize the other one, but she didn't look like she was related to Master Kim.

We turned and bowed in their direction like we were supposed to.

"Class, *charyut!*" Master Kim called, and we stood at attention right where we were standing.

The first thing Master Kim did was line everyone up

by rank. In class, we did this automatically. But at tests, Master Kim had to be sure everyone could be seen by their judge, so the lines were off-centered.

I was surprised to be second-highest rank. Which meant I was second in line. An orange belt named Marco was high rank and bowed everyone in. "Class, *charyut!* [Attention.] *Kyoonyae!* [Bow.]"

We gave the formal greeting. "*Annyeon hashimnikka.*"

"How is everyone today?" Master Kim asked.

"Good, sir!" we said in unison.

He introduced the other people at the table. The judge I didn't know was Master Sanders. She was a fifth-degree black belt visiting from another school.

Master Kim gave us a rare smile. "Are you ready?"

"Yes, sir!"

"I am glad to hear it. No need for luck when you are prepared."

I supposed it was true, but still. Yikes! I wondered if anyone else's stomach flipped.

The test was like a longer version of a class. Well, if the class was being watched and recorded by a few dozen people, and there were three judges who took notes on your every move.

We went through our basic kicks and punches and blocks. Sometimes Master Kim called them out in Korean and other times in English. I only had to peek once at the people next to me to make sure I was doing the right thing.

I concentrated on what I was doing and tried not to

think about everybody watching. (Even though I hated to admit it, it helped that Dad was the only one there.) I wondered what opening night was going to be like. Would the whole cafeteria be full? Would parents be filming that, too? What if I forgot my lines?

Focus! I told myself. *That's a problem for Future Eliza.*

Ha. Future Eliza would be a funny name for a superhero. *There's evil in the world, but don't fear! Future Eliza will save the day . . . tomorrow!*

Rats.

While I was thinking about the play, Master Kim had told everyone to demonstrate their back kicks. I scrambled to catch up without drawing too much attention to myself. That was kind of impossible since Master Kim No. 2 was looking right at me. He wrote something down on his score sheet.

Double rats.

After showing that we knew the basics, we moved on to our self-defense skills. Yellow belts testing for gold had to show they could defend themselves from a shove.

Since Marco and I were about the same height, we paired up. I ran at him first and he moved out of the way easily. Next, he ran at me with his arms ready to shove. I pivoted on my left foot, swung my right to the side and opened like a door.

Perfect!

Hopefully, my judge saw that, too.

A GOOD MARTIAL ARTIST ADAPTS

Next, we were called up to the table a few at a time to do the memorization part of our tests. Master Kim's brother was my judge.

"Yes, sir!" I answered when he called my name. I jumped up, bowed, and hurried to the table.

He gave me a smile. "Good afternoon, Eliza."

"Good afternoon, sir."

I concentrated on a spot on the wall just over his shoulder as he quizzed me.

"What is your uniform called?"

"*Dobok.*"

"How do you say 'Thank you'?"

"*Kamsahhamida.*"

"Where does taekwondo come from?"

This was something I had to know for my yellow-belt test. "South Korea."

Master Kim No. 2 smiled. "Please count to twenty in Korean," he asked.

I knew this! Piece of cake!

"*Hana, dool, set, net, dasut, yasut, ilgop, yuldol, ahop, yul, yul hana, yul dool, yul set, yul net, yul dasut, yul yasut, yul ilgop, yul yuldol, yul ahop, seumul.*"

"Nicely done," Master Kim No. 2 said. "Now please count to thirty."

My brain slammed on the brakes. Count to thirty? That wasn't on my flash cards! Did I forget to study?

Master Kim No. 2 gave me an encouraging nod.

I shifted my weight from side to side. "I'm sorry, sir. I don't know how."

"Yes, you do," Master Kim No. 2 said. "Think about it."

I searched the files in my brain but came up with nothing, nada, zilch.

"Counting to thirty was not on your test requirements," Master Kim No. 2 said. "You do not *have* to know this yet. But a martial artist takes what he or she knows and adapts to solve a problem. So, adapt."

How on earth was I supposed to figure out how to count to thirty?!

I counted to twenty again in my head, hoping the answer would magically come to me. I couldn't see him, but I knew Dad was watching from the sidelines. Probably wondering why it was taking me so long to be dismissed. It was too bad he couldn't telepathically send me a last-minute mnemonic device like he did to help me remember how to count from ten to twenty. (*"Seumul* sounds like Samuel. You don't need *twenty* brothers.")

Wait! Eleven was just ten with a one added—*yul hana.*

I took a chance. *"Seumul hana,"* I said. Master Kim No. 2 motioned for me to continue.

"*Seumul dool, seumul set, seumul net . . .* "

I paused after twenty-nine (*seumul ahop*).

Master Kim No. 2 smiled. "*Seoreun,*" he said. "That's how you say 'thirty.'"

I repeated the word.

"Well done, Eliza."

My cheeks hurt from grinning. "Thank you, sir."

MY BOARD BREAK

The board breaks were last. The students lined up along one side of the room so we could watch each other. Master Kim called Marco up first. Which meant I'd be second since we were going in order of rank.

You may not want to go first when you're auditioning for a play, but going first at a taekwondo test is good. It means you have less time to worry. That didn't help me much, though. Since my brain works at a hundred miles an hour, I'd already (as Dad liked to say) "pushed all the buttons on the Panic Elevator" by the time Marco broke his board on his first attempt.

Master Kim picked up another board from the stack and called my name.

Gulp! Good thing I wasn't supposed to be breaking with a kick, because my legs were rubber bands.

Master Kim held up the board and I adjusted it so it was just right.

"You got this!" Dad called.

"*Go, Eliza!*" Sophia and a few of the color belts yelled.

I got into my ready stance, my hands pulled into a fisted guard.

It's gonna hurt, a voice in my head warned. *Don't do it!*

Master Kim always said to visualize. I tried to ignore the voice and imagined the board as nothing but a giant graham cracker.

I can do this. No problem!

With a *kihap,* I raised my right hand into a hammer fist and brought it down on the board.

Owwwwwww!

I opened my eyes.

The board wasn't broken.

Master Kim nodded. "Try again," he commanded.

I lined up the board/giant graham cracker again.

"*Huuup!*"

But my hand hit the board with a thud. I shook my hand, trying to shake off the pain.

"You have one more attempt," Master Kim reminded me.

I nodded.

"Take a moment if you need it," Master Kim said.

I didn't need a moment. I needed ice! And maybe a more cooperative board.

The butterflies in my stomach were fluttering like mad. And hot tears pricked my eyes. What if I couldn't break the board? A boy at my first test couldn't break his board and Master Kim made him sit down. Madison said he'd get another chance during class. But he didn't get his new belt that day.

I wanted my gold belt. Today.

I looked at Dad, who gave me an encouraging smile. Then, out of the corner of my eye, I saw Master Kim No. 2. I remembered what he'd said about a martial artist taking what they know and adapting.

Okay. Here's what I knew:

Imagining the board being easy to break wasn't working. My hand hurt. A lot.

I hadn't practiced my hammer fist with my left hand. So switching hands was out.

Suddenly, a lightning-bolt idea came to me.

If imagining the board as something weak wasn't working, then maybe I needed to imagine my hand as something strong!

I lined myself back up and took a deep breath. Then I drew all my power from my *danjun*. My energy wasn't red, like Master Kim had suggested that day in class.

Mine was silver. Like the top of a hammer.

My *hand* was a hammer.

"*Huuup!*"

TA-DA!

And just like that, I was a gold belt.

A NICE BRUISE

After Master Kim handed out the new belts, Marco bowed us out.

"*Hae sahn*, class dismissed," Master Kim said. "And congratulations!"

Everybody's families crowded us for hugs and pictures. Dad admired my new belt. "Gold suits you," he said.

He held up his hand for me to high-five, but I shook my head.

Master Kim strolled over and handed me an ice pack. "Here. I thought you might need one of these."

"Thank you, sir."

"How is your hand?" he asked. I showed it to him.

"That will have a nice bruise by tomorrow," he said.

"As opposed to a mean bruise?" I asked. I wanted to take it back the second it was out of my mouth. But Master Kim and Dad laughed. So I did, too.

BAD ENOUGH

Mom and Sam got home a little after nine that night. Mom gave me a big hug, congratulated me on my new belt, and then examined my hand. "Good news," she said. "You'll live." Afterwards she announced she was exhausted and headed to bed.

Sam went to the kitchen to make himself a sandwich and I followed.

"How'd the test go?" he asked.

I told him all about it.

"That's good. So, uh. I really am sorry about missing it. I think it's cool you're still taking classes and stuff."

I eyeballed him. Sam wasn't the kind of brother who usually apologized for stuff. Not even that one time he told me there was a snow day, so I turned off my alarm and then Mom yelled at me for sleeping in. Maybe I could use his guilt to my advantage.

"If you feel so bad about missing the belt test," I said carefully, "just think how bad you'll feel about missing the play."

Sam scowled at me as he slapped cheese on his sandwich. "I'm not skipping the dance," he said.

"Why?"

"Because I'm not."

"You don't even like dancing."

"That's true," he admitted. "But I like Megan."

"More than you like me?"

Sam sighed. "You're my sister. She's my girlfriend."

"There's only one opening night," I tried. "It's not like there won't be a bunch of other dances. Can't you miss *one*?"

"I can't."

"You mean you won't."

"Fine. I won't. Happy?"

"No."

Sam added lettuce and the second slice of bread. His voice got quiet. "It doesn't mean I don't feel bad about it, though."

"Just not bad enough," I said.

"Nope," he said. "Not bad enough."

I wasn't a quitter, but I knew when I was beat.

PINKIES

It was Monday. Opening night was four days away. It was good my gold-belt test was over, because we had rehearsals every day now. I would have to miss taekwondo classes, but Master Kim said he understood.

The crew was finally finished with the sets. The barn set everyone had painted was the biggest.

"I need all hands on deck," Mrs. Delany called. "The barn wall is too big to go up the stairs, so we've gotta hoist it up to the stage."

Everyone started moving to the cafeteria floor, where

the crew had laid the set so we could grab an edge. Annie was on the other side of the barn wall. With Paige. I could see their fake diamond earrings from across the room. She hadn't hung out with me during rehearsal since the night I'd said I wanted to do the new ad-libbed line. At lunch, we stuck to complaining about homework and teachers.

JJ slid in next to me. "'Hoist' is a great word, isn't it?" he said. "It rhymes with 'joist,' and that's on my Top Ten list of favorite words to say."

Vivian and I rolled our eyes.

"What's one of your favorites?" JJ asked us.

"Favorite what?" Vivian answered.

"Words to say."

Vivian thought it about it. "'Pumpernickel' is fun, I suppose."

"'Nougat,'" I said.

JJ grinned. "Ooo. 'Nougat' is a good one!"

Mrs. Delany started barking instructions. "Don't bunch together. Make sure you're evenly spaced. Okay, squat down. *Don't* bend! Lift with your *legs*. Calling your parents and explaining that you hurt your back because you didn't follow directions isn't on my list of things to do today."

I got into position. JJ was to one side of me, and Vivian was to the other. We did squats in taekwondo, so doing them now wasn't a big deal. But some people moaned and groaned. Surprisingly, Paige wasn't one of them. In fact, she was right in the middle of things, helping to lift the set.

"One, two, three, lift!" Mrs. Delany called.

The wall wasn't so heavy with everyone helping. I had a solid grip, but to the left of me, JJ adjusted his hand until it was next to mine.

Holy smokes. Our pinkies are touching. Does he notice?

I glanced at JJ and he smiled. It was just his regular smile. Nothing weird. But he didn't move his hand.

Is he leaving his hand there on purpose? Or is it just too risky to change positions again since we're moving?

Arg.

Cole, who was wearing a shirt that said STAGE MAN-AGER, crawled under the wall and pushed from the middle so we could raise it up to the stage. After we slid it onstage and raised it into position against the backstage wall, Vivian pulled me aside.

"I think JJ likes you," she whispered.

"Yeah?"

She nodded and smiled. I was so confused about it all that I told Vivian about the pinkies.

"Did you feel electricity? My sister's in college and says you're supposed to feel electricity when someone you like touches you."

I shrugged. "I don't know. It just felt warm."

Vivian put her hands on her hips. "Warm's a start!"

THE PART WHERE I TRIED AGAIN (BECAUSE BEST FRIENDS TRY)

I approached Annie at our break. "That barn set was heavy, huh?" I said.

"Yeah. A little."

"Did you have a good weekend?"

"I guess. I mostly just ran lines and stuff like that."

I didn't bother asking who she ran lines with since I already had a pretty good idea.

"Guess what? I passed my gold-belt test on Saturday."

Annie brightened and gave me a hug. "Wow! Congrats!"

Finally! We were getting on the right track.

"Check out my war wound," I said, holding up my hand to show her my bruise. (Master Kim was right; it was a pretty nice one. It looked like a galaxy.)

"Oh my goodness! What happened to you?" Mrs. Delany asked, coming up behind us. She gently grabbed my hand to examine it.

"It's nothing."

"Please tell me that didn't happen when we were moving the set earlier."

"No, no," I told her. "It's from my taekwondo test over the weekend. I had a little trouble with my board break is all. But it's fine. Really. It only looks bad."

Mrs. Delany breathed a sigh. "Thank heavens." She smiled. "I didn't know you did martial arts. What belt level are you at?"

"I just tested for my gold belt," I told her.

"That's fabulous!" She leaned in closer. "I did karate in college. I got all the way to my purple belt."

"No way! Really?" I said. Mrs. Delany nodded.

Annie sighed. "I gotta go," she said.

BREAK A LEG

Later that night, I sat on my bedroom floor and tried to work on my homework. But I kept thinking about Annie.

Clearly, she was upset about something. Maybe she was just tired from the long rehearsals; we all were. But I didn't think that was it. And it was strange how she left so suddenly when Mrs. Delany and I started talking about martial arts. What had I done to make her mad? Operation BBF was going downhill. At top speed.

Now, Paige was a different story. I knew exactly why she was mad at me. But that one wasn't my fault. It wasn't like I set out to embarrass her when the set door got stuck.

Or planned out the snouty-snout-snout line. Those things just happened. I guess she had a point about the play being her big break, though. Was I really ruining it? It was one new line.

"Knock, knock," Dad said from my bedroom doorway. "Got a sec?"

I shoved my books aside. "Sure."

As he walked in, Dad pulled something from behind his back. "Here. I made you a present."

It was a wooden board with my name painted on it. Below that top board, two long, thin boards hung horizontally. It reminded me of a very short rope ladder. My white belt and yellow belt were folded and secured to the lower boards with elastic bands.

"I figured we can add a new board with each new belt," Dad said.

I jumped up and hugged him. "It's awesome! Thank you!"

Dad grinned. "I wanted to do something nice for you. I'm glad you like it."

"I really do," I told him. "Where should I hang it?"

Dad and I hung the belt rack over my desk. That way, I could always see how far I'd come. I only had three belts so far (two on the rack and one that I wore) but it made me feel good that Dad believed I could make it all the way to my black belt someday.

After Dad left, I took a break from my homework. The belt rack had inspired me. Maybe all I needed to do to fix things with Annie was to do something nice for her. And it would be nice to do something for the rest of the cast and crew, too. After all, best friends did nice things for each other for no particular reason.

I knew just the thing. Cupcakes!

It was a little tricky doubling the cake batter recipe, but I managed. I had to make sure not to turn the mixer on high so the batter didn't come splashing out.

Next, I used a measuring cup to scoop my batter into cupcake liners. In one of her TV-show episodes, Sweet Caroline said she liked using measuring cups for batter because then everything was even.

I turned the muffin pan halfway through the bake time (like Sweet Caroline does) and then set the cupcakes out on the kitchen table to cool. I even moved the chairs away so Bear wouldn't jump up and eat all my hard work.

I got out my recipe for fluffy frosting. It was my favorite even though it took forever. First I had to cook the sugar, water, and cream of tartar on the stovetop. Then I had to whip the egg whites and vanilla, add the sugar mixture, and beat it for ten minutes, until stiff peaks formed. I chose green food coloring and added extra because green is Annie's favorite color.

Next, I got the piping bags and decorating tips that Mom found at Goodwill and used them to frost the cupcakes. By the time I was done, my hands ached from all the squeezing. Afterward, Sam helped me find a box and line it with foil so I could carry the cupcakes to school. Dad said he would drop them off when he drove over to school to give me my medication. Now that rehearsals were going longer and I really needed to focus, I was taking one of my quick-acting pills in the afternoon.

I stood back and admired my handiwork. The cupcakes looked good.

But not great. They were missing something.

On a cupcake show I liked to watch, they always have a decoration round. So even though it was almost bedtime, I baked a double batch of sugar cookies. I used my cookie cutter that looked like a Christmas stocking and frosted them with a white glaze.

"What are those?" Mom asked when she saw them.

"Casts!" I told her.

She looked confused for a minute. Then she figured it out. "Ah! I get it!" she said. "Break a leg! That's clever."

I smiled and took a bow.

"THEY'RE CUPCAKES."

Even with the halls mostly empty, maneuvering the box of cupcakes after school was a challenge. Thankfully, someone was around to open the door to the cafeteria for me.

I walked over to the snack table and carefully slid the cupcakes onto one end. I couldn't wait for everyone to see what I'd made. Especially Annie. I'd told her I had a surprise for her. She was curious.

At snack time, I darted over to the table before everyone else and pulled off the foil cover. I was careful not to rip it so I could save it for later. I didn't think I'd need it, though. I'd made just enough cupcakes for everyone to have one.

"What are those for?" Paige asked, eyeing my box.

"They're for fun. They're cupcakes."

"I know what cupcakes look like," she said. "I mean, it was Monica's turn to bring snacks."

I saw that Monica had already spread out a plate of cheese and crackers and fruit. People were making themselves plates.

"We'll just have more snacks, then," I said, and smiled.

"That's inconsiderate to Monica, don't you think?" Paige asked.

205

I looked at Monica. "I'm sorry. I just thought it would be a nice surprise. I didn't mean to butt in."

Paige made a *humph* sound.

"I don't mind. They look good," Monica said. "Are those supposed to be casts?"

I beamed. "Yep! You know, like 'break a leg.'"

"I can't wait to try one," Monica said. Paige shot her a warning look.

"Well, I'm not eating any," Paige announced. "Look at all that gross green frosting. It'll stain my mouth for sure."

"It won't stain," I told her. Even though I wasn't sure if that was true or not. (I *had* used almost half a bottle of food coloring.)

"The play is only three days away. I don't know about anyone else, but *I'm* not taking any chances," Paige said as she helped herself to cheese cubes and fruit slices.

A few minutes later, I sat down to eat with JJ and Vivian. When I looked over at Annie, I noticed she'd taken a cupcake. *Yay!* She saw me watching and gave me a smile.

But when she thought I wasn't looking anymore, she scraped off the cookie and frosting and picked a few bites off the top of cake part before covering her plate with a napkin.

I felt like a fallen soufflé.

GOOD THING I KEPT THE FOIL

After rehearsal, I went over to the snack table to help clean up. I figured I'd just throw the cupcake box out. Only it was still half full.

AT LUNCH ON WEDNESDAY

The cupcakes were good," Annie said.

"Thanks," I replied. I thought she might tell me she had changed her mind and was done hanging out with Paige for good.

But she didn't. She did the next best thing, though.

"Wanna work on our list?" she asked. She pulled out the Rules to Surviving Sixth Grade notebook.

We came up with a new one and she wrote it down. No. 37: The bathroom near the art room is always cold.

I was in the middle of brainstorming another when Annie said, "I've been thinking about the Paige thing. About her wanting you to ask Mrs. Delany to ditch the new line."

"You said I should do what I want."

"Yeah, but I changed my mind," Annie said as she doodled on the cover of the notebook. "I think Paige made a good point. It's distracting."

"What changed your mind?" I asked. "Did Paige get to you?"

"Nobody *got* to me," Annie said. "I can think for myself."

"So why did you change your mind?'

"I just did, all right?" she said.

Skunk stew. This was *not* how I wanted things to be going. I wanted the two of us to be sitting here, eating our lunches, and writing in our notebook. And definitely *not* talking about Paige. Again.

"It isn't up to me," I told Annie. "Mrs. Delany is the director."

"Yeah, but she might listen to you. Say you don't want to do it."

"Can we talk about something else?" I said.

Annie put a big bite of mashed potatoes in her mouth.

"What did you do last night?" I asked to get things rolling.

Annie swallowed her food and seemed to brighten a bit. "I added more curlers to my wig. I want to make a funnier entrance, and my book says audiences like visual humor."

Okay. It was still about the play but at least we weren't talking about you-know-who anymore.

"That'll be funny," I told her. "Well, funnier. Your entrance already gets a laugh."

It was true. In Act Three, after Paige said "This barn is a-bustin' and this party is a-poppin'," Annie stepped onstage and said, "No. It's a rumpus!" while wearing her lime-green bathrobe and kitten slippers.

Annie's entrance was a very important part of the play, too. Her character calls the sheriff because of all the party noise, and when the sheriff shows up, he brings his son along. And that's the guy Cinder Ellen saw in town earlier and has a crush on. So, really, there was no happily-ever-after without Annie.

I reminded Annie of this.

"Yeah," she said. "But my entrance still isn't as funny as the snout line."

Whoa. Hold the donuts. I can't believe I didn't see it before!

"Annie, are you jealous?" I asked her.

"What? No!"

"Are you sure?" I asked.

"Yes!"

"You're acting like it," I told her.

"No I'm not."

"You are too. That's why you want me to ask Mrs. Delany to leave out the ad-lib. You're afraid it'll get a bigger laugh than your entrance."

"I can't believe you said that," Annie fumed.

"I'm not even in the scene when you come onstage," I told her. "No one will remember the funny thing I said."

"It doesn't matter," Annie said.

"Why can't we both be funny?" I asked her.

"Because I'm the one who cares about it," she said, her voice rising. "It was my idea to audition for the play in the first place. *I'm* the one who wants to be a professional actor someday. You just tagged along."

"Because you *begged* me to."

Annie scoffed and then she shoved the Rules to Surviving Sixth Grade notebook at me. "Here! I don't want this anymore."

I pushed it back.

"Fine," Annie said. She got up and grabbed the notebook off the table. I followed her as she marched over to one of the giant trash cans by the exit and threw the notebook in.

"Don't be such a diva," I said.

Annie whirled around to face me. "Oh. *I'm* being a diva?"

"Yeah," I told her. "You kinda are."

Annie pointed her finger at me and her face grew dark. "You know what you are? You're a black cloud that follows me around and ruins *everything*. Everybody was right. Nimbus is the perfect name for you!"

YIN, NO YANG

I told the nurse that I had a really bad headache, and she called Dad to come pick me up from school.

"Can I get you anything?" Dad asked. When we got home, he had set me up on the couch. I shook my head. Pillows and blankets weren't going to help. Neither was the ice pack that Dad brought me. The pain wasn't in my head.

"I'm just in the other room if you need anything," Dad said as he closed the curtains. He had to finish homework for one of his classes. "I'll bring you something to eat in a bit."

I was pretty sure I'd never want to eat again. After Annie left, I thought about digging out our notebook. I didn't know why I still wanted it, but I did. But before I could grab it, some boy walked over to the garbage can and scraped off his leftovers. And then dumped out the rest of his milk carton for good measure.

The notebook was gone. One big, soggy mess. Just like Operation BBF. Who was I going to talk to before homeroom or in the hall? Who would care when something funny happened or help me with my taekwondo flash cards? Who was I going to eat lunch with?

It wasn't just that I'd be lonely. I was going to miss Annie.

I used the corner of the fuzzy blanket Dad brought me to wipe the corners of my eyes. The blanket made me think about Annie's kitten slippers. And the play.

The thought of having to be around her for dress rehearsal and the shows after she'd called me *that name* made my throat ache.

I still couldn't believe she'd said it. The worst part wasn't the nickname, either. It was her telling me I was a dark cloud that ruined everything. Maybe it was true. I mean, I'd ruined the chemistry lab. I'd ruined things with Tony. And now I'd ruined things with her.

I should quit the play, I thought. I'll probably ruin it, too. Someone else could take my place. Or maybe the show could just have two little pigs, instead of three. It's a weird, mishmash play anyway. I could tell Mrs. Delany I'm sick.

I hid under the covers and tried to be quiet so Dad wouldn't find out I was crying.

Mom gently shook me awake a while later. She was still wearing her hospital scrubs and smelled faintly of rubbing alcohol.

"Hey, sweetie," she said. "How's my favorite girl in the world feeling?"

I pushed myself up. "Okay," I said, even though my eyes felt puffy. I was sure my nose was red, too.

"Headache better?" Mom asked as she studied my face.

"Yeah," I said. Except now I kinda had a real headache from crying. "Wait. Is it nighttime?"

Mom shook her head. "No. My boss let me clock out half an hour early is all."

"You didn't have to come just for me," I told her. (Now I felt even worse about faking with the school nurse.)

"Of course I did," Mom said. "I have to make sure you're better in time for opening night."

"So you're definitely coming?" I asked.

"With a bright shiny face and a camera!" Mom said.

After she left to put the ice pack away, I thought more about it. Sam wasn't coming to the opening night. But Mom and Dad were. I didn't want to disappoint them. Plus, there was JJ and Vivian to think about. They'd probably be disappointed. And if I bailed on the play, it might make things harder for them. Mrs. Delany would be disappointed, too. She said my ad-libbed line was her all-time favorite.

It was *my* favorite line in the play, too.

I was really looking forward to being onstage with JJ and Vivian. And to saying my funny new line. If I quit, *I'd* be disappointed. I might have auditioned because Annie wanted me to, but it turned out I really liked theater. And I was good at it. I worked just as hard as everyone else and I deserved to be there on opening night. So even though Annie had said what she said, I was going to enjoy my moment in the spotlight. After all, a good martial artist never quits.

DRESS REHEARSAL

After warm-ups, Mrs. Delany had everyone gather for a pep talk. Annie was on the other side of the stage standing with Paige and Monica. She wouldn't even look in my direction.

"This is it, friends!" Mrs. Delany said. "We have one final rehearsal before the big show. So get all the mess-ups and flub-dubs out of your system now."

We were doing the show as if there was an audience. Costumes, makeup, set changes, everything. So Mrs. Delany told us to keep going. No matter what. And stay in character.

Cole cued the stage crew to open the curtain, and the "show" started.

I don't know what happened. Maybe Mrs. Delany telling us to get our mistakes over with jinxed us. But it was a disaster.

Here's a small list of some of the things that went wrong:

People mumbled lines.

Someone backstage sneezed—loudly—in the middle of a scene.

The curtain opened too soon and a stage ninja had to duck behind a hay bale and stay there until the curtain closed again.

The guy running the spotlight had trouble aiming it.

Someone's shoe was untied and he tripped coming onstage.

The stage crew rushed through the scene change for the farmer's house and forgot the phone, so the characters onstage had to pretend instead.

By the time it came for me, JJ, and Vivian to do our first scene, we were running *way* behind schedule. I knew this because Cole kept pointing at his watch and Mrs. Delany was out where the audience would be, pacing.

I adjusted my pig-ears headband and made sure the buttons on my shirt were all buttoned. JJ, Vivian, and I had matching Western-style shirts. My fancy blue dress was for the party scene.

Everyone positioned themselves onstage and the curtain opened.

A tingling feeling traveled through my toes and up my body. Being onstage was so different now that everybody was in costume and the spotlights were shining.

JJ, Vivian, and I pretended to shop and talk to each other. Pretty soon it was time for Paige to get "stuck" in the flower shop. There were a few bumps like someone was trying to open the door. Then Paige cried, "Someone let me out!"

I said my new line. Even though there wasn't an audience there to laugh, I felt like I'd just broken a board. Or two boards at the same time!

At the end of rehearsal, everyone sat on the stage. Actually, collapsed is more like it.

"Thank you all for hanging in there," Mrs. Delany said. "I appreciate everyone's patience and enthusiasm. I have just a few notes."

As Mrs. Delany started going through the list on her clipboard, I noticed there was a loose thread on the ribbon of my blue dress. I tugged it. Whoops. Bad idea. I sat on my hands to keep them from unraveling the entire piece of gold ribbon. That would have been bad. So long, good omen.

Mrs. Delany ended the afternoon by telling us her favorite theater superstition: a bad dress rehearsal meant a great opening. "So I look forward to a successful show tomorrow. Now go home and get to bed early, friends!"

OPENING NIGHT

So, yea or nay on the hot dogs?" Dad asked, holding the refrigerator door open.

I shifted my chin to the other hand and sighed. "Yeah, I guess."

Dad grinned. "Wieners are the winner!"

I had to give him credit. He was doing his best to cheer me up about the news we'd gotten: Mom wasn't coming to opening night. There was a huge car accident on the highway and it was all hands on deck at the hospital. "I'm so sorry, Eliza!" Mom said as she headed out the door. "I'll do my best to be there before the curtain opens."

She wouldn't make it. She almost never made it back on time when she got called in for an emergency shift. One time, when I was six and she'd missed one of my soccer games, I told her it was "the worst day of my whole life." And then Mom explained that the people she'd helped were having a very bad day, too. I felt guilty. I still felt guilty. Even though I knew it wasn't her fault, I was sad she was missing the play.

I looked around the table: Sam, Dad, and me. There was always someone missing, it seemed. It wasn't always the same person, but we were always minus one. Even opening night couldn't bring us together. My plan was ruined.

Sam was going to a dinner party at Megan's house before the dance, but he hadn't left yet. He wanted some of the mac-and-cheese with hot dogs. (He wasn't worried about ruining his appetite; he was always hungry.) Dad had offered to take me to a fast-food hamburger place to celebrate, but I was afraid the greasy food would make me throw up. I'd been nerv-ited all day. (FYI, nervous + excited = nerv-ited.)

"Time to carb up!" Dad said, placing the bowl of mac-and-cheese-and-wieners in front of me.

"I'm not running a marathon," I told him.

"I don't know," he teased. "Maybe the play will be so terrible that the audience revolts and chases the actors into the street."

"Jeez, D!" Sam said. "Way to plant an image in her head."

Dad shrugged. Then he told one of his lame jokes: "What did the one hot dog say to the other hot dog? See you later! Hope we can *ketchup* soon!" Sam and I groaned.

After dinner, Dad gave me my medication. Sam took

a shower and put on his suit. Dad took pictures for Mom and made Sam promise to have someone take more of him and Megan together later on. It was nearly time for us to leave for school, too.

"Last chance to bail on the dance and come see the play," I told Sam.

"Last chance to give it a rest," he answered. But I could tell he wasn't mad.

Dad took a few more pictures for Mom.

"Oh shoot!" Sam said. "Almost forgot." He bolted to the kitchen and returned with two boxes that I'd seen in the fridge earlier.

"This one's Megan's," he said, setting the square box aside. "But this one is for you, E." I took the long box he held out. Inside was a small bouquet of pink roses and baby's breath tied with a ribbon.

"I saw them when I was picking up Megan's wrist corsage. I wasn't sure what color to get. I hope you like pink."

I stared at him.

"What?" Sam said to me. "You can't have an opening night without flowers. It's a rule or something."

"Thank you!" I said, hugging him.

"Hey. Watch the suit! I don't want it to wrinkle." Sam checked his buzzing phone. "My ride's here."

"Have fun," Dad told him. "Make good choices."

"Yeah, have fun," I told him. And I meant it. If he could be thoughtful, then so could I.

Sam turned to me. "Sorry again I can't go to the play."

He paused and then smirked. "But break a leg this time, not your butt!"

GETTING READY

The cafeteria didn't look like a cafeteria anymore. It looked like a theater.

The lights were dimmed and there were chairs lined up in rows in front of the stage. There was even a ticket table with a fancy tablecloth and a poster of the script's cover near the entrance. And there were playbills on the table for people to take. Real, live playbills! (I didn't know what a playbill was until JJ explained it to me. Basically, it was a fancy program with the cast and crew's pictures and biographies.)

I picked up one of the playbills and leafed through it until I found the bio I had had to write for myself a few weeks ago:

Eliza Bing is a sixth grader and is excited to be playing one of the Three Little Pigs because that was one of her favorite stories when she was little. This is her first production.

It felt kinda weird writing about myself in third person. The bios weren't supposed to be more than three sentences, although Paige and other people with big roles got to write a paragraph. The part about the Three Little Pigs being one my favorite stories was sorta true. Actually, it was a book called *The True Story of the 3 Little Pigs!* as told to Jon Scieszka. FYI, the wolf had a very different perspective.

Call time, when everybody had to check in with Mrs. Delany, was at 6:45 sharp. Excitement jumped back and forth between everyone like static electricity. Mrs. D made sure we were all there and then gave us the pre-show pep talk because she said it'd be too chaotic to do it later.

"Welcome to opening night, friends! This is my favorite part of theater! Our hard work is behind us and now it's time to reap the reward. Remember, we're a family, which means love and respect and all that jazz until strike do us part. If you miss a line, keep going. The show must go on!"

"So go out there, do your best," said Mrs. Delany. "And, most importantly, have fun!"

Mrs. Delany had us snap our fingers twice. It was her own pre-show superstition, she explained. Afterward, we headed to our dressing rooms—which were really just classrooms that were near the backstage door. I was on one side of the girls' dressing room with the rest of the ensemble. Annie was on the other side of the room.

Remembering how she called me Nimbus made me feel like I was wearing a wet coat. But I shoved it off; I had to get ready and I was there to enjoy the night.

Vivian and I got dressed in our Western shirts and helped each other adjust our piggy-ear headbands. Someone from the makeup crew helped us paint our faces pink and handed out pig snouts to put on later. "Don't lose these," she warned.

Cole popped in after everyone was changed. "The house

is open and curtain is in thirty minutes. Break a leg and have fun, everyone," he told us. "The parent volunteer has a headset, so let me know if there's an emergency. Someone will come get you when it gets close to your turn to go on. Otherwise, stay put."

There was nothing to do but wait. Vivian and I played Hangman on the whiteboard with a bunch of other people.

Mrs. Delany had collected all our cell phones ("Too distracting!"), so I checked the clock on the wall: 7:52. The play started in eight minutes.

THE PART WHERE I BREAK THE RULES A LITTLE

I told the parent watching the door that I had to use the bathroom. Instead, I snuck down the dark hall and up into the wings of the stage. Everyone in the first act was quietly milling around, waiting for the curtain. Some people were fidgeting. Others were pacing or looking at their scripts one last time. Paige was off to one side, alone. She had her eyes closed and was taking deep breaths. It reminded me of how we meditated at taekwondo. She looked calm.

No one paid attention to me as I crept to the edge of

stage left. I hoped everyone in the audience was busy reading their playbills or looking at their phones as I carefully pulled back the heavy curtain the tiniest bit.

My left knee shook. I scanned the audience as quickly as I could. Oh man! Was Dad running late?

I let out the air in my lungs when I finally found him. He was in the sixth row on the right side of the house.

The seat next to him was empty.

BRIGHT LIGHTS, JELLY LEGS

Cole put his finger up to his lips and ushered us through the backstage door. The fairy-tale and nursery-rhyme characters ensemble was about to go out for the first time.

JJ held out his hands to me and Vivian, and the three of us did a simultaneous fist bump. It was too quick to notice any electricity between me and JJ. Plus, all I was thinking about was whether or not my jelly legs would hold me up for much longer.

We hurried onstage and took our places while the curtain was closed. No one in the audience was talking, but you could hear people rustling about and a couple of fold-up chairs squeaking.

I adjusted my snout and took a deep breath. But it felt like my chest was hollow and there wasn't enough air in the world to fill it. Cole cued the stagehands, and the curtain opened.

My brain froze but thankfully my body remembered where to go. It was a farm scene, and pretty much all I had to do was wander around in the background until Anthony (Mr. Goat) walked past and fake-sneezed. A minute or so into the scene, he did.

"*Achoo!*"

"Gesundheit!" I said.

I couldn't believe how strange (and really loud) my voice sounded in the big room. But it was also cool to have everyone listening to me.

Being onstage was amazing! I didn't have any more lines in that act, so I got to relax and watch the other actors. It was like having a front-row seat to the play.

Without being too obvious, I scanned the audience again. I counted the rows and found Dad. Now there was someone next to him! Mom had made it after all! A camera was in front of her face.

I waited patiently for her to look over so I could smile or sneak in a wave. But then . . .

Nope.

The lady moved the camera. And then scooted over to the next seat. She'd only been looking for a better shot of her own kid.

I'd been right. Mom wasn't going to make it. Dad caught me looking his way and gave me a thumbs-up.

It didn't help.

IN WHICH IT'S TIME FOR MY BIG LINE

There was nothing I could do but hope that Dad would be able to tell Mom about my performance. And since Mrs. Delany said the show must go on, I got ready.

My next scene was coming up. It was the one where the fairy-tale characters were walking around shops, doing our thing, while Cinder Ellen (Paige) went into the dry-cleaning shop to pick up her stepmother's dress for the Barnyard Bash. It was also the scene where Cinder Ellen sees the sheriff's son and develops a crush.

The *shuuuush-shuuuush* of the curtain opening, the bright, warm lights on my face, and the buzz of being onstage again were just as strong and thrilling as the first time. Even if Mom wasn't there.

Vivian, JJ, and I stood in the "street," near the stick vendor.

"Straw is superb," JJ said, holding up a fistful of hay.

Vivian shook her head. "Silly boy. Sticks would be stupendous."

I stamped my foot like a toddler and said my line. "No! Bricks are best!"

There was a smattering of laughter. It felt great, like jumping into a pool on a hot day. I couldn't wait to hear the audience's reaction to my new line.

I had a few minutes before Paige got "stuck" in the shop. JJ, Vivian, and I continued to quietly fake-argue about building materials. Mostly it involved JJ making funny faces at us (since his back was to the audience) and me and Vivian trying not to break character.

My big moment was getting closer.

I started thinking about Paige's trying to get me to drop the ad-libbed line. Which made me mad. And then I thought about Annie's being so jealous that she threw away our Rules to Surviving notebook and called me a dark rain cloud that ruined everything. Which made me even madder. But even if I wanted to (and I didn't), I couldn't skip the line now. It wasn't about me, or me getting laughs. It would mess up the scene.

Rob, the boy who played the farmer's son, walked across the stage.

This is it. Get ready!

"Hot diggity! The e-vites go out today," Rob said.

Paige was going to rattle the door and say, "Oh my. The door is stuck. Somebody let me out."

And I was going to say, "Not by the hair of my snouty snout snout!" Everyone was going to laugh before Rob walked over and saved the day.

Only that's not what happened.

Paige opened the set door, breezed onto the stage, and went on with the scene.

My line stuck in my throat like a wad of bread. JJ's eyes grew wide. Vivian gave me a sympathetic look.

I kept my poker face until the end of the act. Right before the curtain closed all the way, I caught a glimpse of Dad in the audience. Mom was sitting next to him, this time for real.

INTERMISSION

Back in the dressing room, Paige and her gang gushed about the first half of the play. I sent Vivian to eavesdrop.

"Okay," Vivian said when she got back. "Paige claimed that she just forgot. She said her brain was on autopilot and since it wasn't originally in the script . . ."

Vivian let Paige's lie sink in.

"I'm sorry you didn't get to do your line," Vivian told me. "You'd've nailed it."

My eyes wandered over to Annie, who was still standing near Paige. Her eyes flickered in my direction.

"Forget about it," Vivian said. "Let's get ready."

THE ONLY RULE TO BEING A BEST FRIEND

I didn't have any lines in the Barnyard Bash scene. My job was to hang out in the background with the rest of the ensemble on the hay bales.

In my other scenes, it'd been fun watching the rest of the cast perform. But it wasn't anymore. I felt like a voodoo doll Paige had stabbed with long needles. I wondered if Mrs. Delany would say something to her about skipping the line. Even if she got in trouble for it and Mrs. Delany told her to do the line tomorrow, Mom wouldn't get to see it.

The sound guy cued the music and everyone got up to dance. JJ did this funny move he called the "sprinkler" and it made me and Vivian laugh. (Which was okay, since we were at a party.) And at least I got to wear my blue dress with the lucky gold ribbon that matched my new gold belt.

I could see Annie waiting in the wings, ready for her cue. She'd added bows to her kitten slippers. She was definitely going to get the big laugh she wanted when she waltzed onstage. But I didn't have time to worry about Annie. A girl named Debbie jumped on top of a hay bale, and that was everyone's cue to take the dancing and laughter up a notch.

Paige was downstage, saying her monologue. Rob, the farmer's son, interrupted her to lock elbows, and swung her around to the music.

Rob was supposed to interrupt her. The thing was, he did it too soon. Paige's eyes grew wide but she stopped saying her lines to dance because that's what she was supposed to do—keep going no matter what. If you were in the audience, you probably wouldn't notice anything out of the ordinary. But the rest of us onstage were like, *Uh-oh.*

The music kept playing. Paige kept twirling. Rob gave her a tiny nod. From the wings, Cole was mouthing *"Next line!"*

Paige plastered a smile on her face, but her eyes gave it away. She was panicking. Big-time.

Finally, Paige's brain kicked back in and she said something.

Only it wasn't her next line. And what was even worse—she'd skipped us ahead by a whole scene!

Cole shoved the boys playing the sheriff and his son onto the stage.

Those of us in the ensemble looked around at each other. We weren't supposed to be onstage during this scene. Now what?

I could see Annie still offstage. She looked like she was about to cry. Without Paige's cue, she'd missed her entrance. And now that we were ahead, she wouldn't even get to be in the show at all.

Even though I was mad at her and she'd hurt me, I felt

bad for Annie. She was excited about being onstage. This was gonna be her big moment.

I thought about my last big moment, at my gold-belt test. I'd been excited, too. And nervous. I remembered what Master Kim No. 2 had said: a good martial artist takes what he or she knows and adapts to solve a problem.

Okay. Here's what I knew: we were in serious trouble onstage.

Here's what I also knew: blurting things out usually got me in trouble. But sometimes it didn't.

And here's the final thing I knew: Mrs. Delany said if anything went wrong, to just keep going. The number one rule in theater was "The show must go on."

I glanced over to Annie. Maybe we weren't friends anymore, but she'd been the one to get me here onstage in the first place. She deserved saving. And so did everyone else in the cast.

So forget rules! Following the rules hadn't gotten me anywhere the last few months. You didn't need rules to survive sixth grade. And it turned out there weren't any magic rules to being a best best friend.

Well, okay, there was *one* rule. And I suddenly knew what it was.

"Excuse me," I said loudly. Everyone's eyes locked on me, and I was sure you could hear my heartbeat way in the back of the audience.

I turned to Vivian. "Didn't you say the hay was making your allergies act up?"

She looked confused.

"And so you made an appointment. . . ." I prompted, and held my breath.

It took her a second, but Vivian's eyes lit up when she finally got it.

"Oh yes! Thank you for reminding me." She turned to Paige and the rest of the cast downstage. "I have a doctor's appointment. I'd better run."

She hurried offstage.

It was the perfect improv. *Thank you for getting it!* I told her telepathically.

JJ grinned and went next. "Please pardon me as well, friends," he ad-libbed. "But I need to shampoo and style my snout hair. I'm entering a pig-stache contest."

He twirled his imaginary snout-stache and dashed offstage.

One by one, everyone in the ensemble improv-ed some excuse for needing to leave. People tried to outdo the person before them.

"I have a major headache," Jack said, holding his head. "I feel like someone threw me down a hill!"

"And I seem to have busted my water pail. I need a new one," his sister Jill said.

"Ooo. Check it out. I just got a text that the pillow I wanted is in stock," Pooped Piper announced. "Gotta go."

"I promised my mom I'd pull weeds," Jack Beanstalk said. "There's a really big one in our front yard!" (This got a huge laugh from the audience.)

"I've got to scramble to work!" Humpty Grumpty said.

"And I'm late picking up my *kid* from soccer practice!" Mr. Goat said.

Eventually all the people who were supposed to be offstage were offstage. I was the only one left.

"I should be saying good night as well," I said. "B.B. Wolf is coming over for dinner and I need to get . . . ready." (I made air quotes over this last part.)

The audience roared and I headed offstage. But at the last second, I stopped.

"Hey Sheriff," I said, addressing the boy with the badge. "If you don't mind me asking, who called you about the party?"

Annie stepped onstage. "That would be me!"

AFTER THE SHOW

The fairy-tale and nursery-rhyme characters were the first to take a bow. We lined up in small groups. I went out with JJ and Vivian and the three of us grabbed hands, raised them up, and leaned over in unison. I still couldn't tell if there was electricity. JJ's hand was mostly just sweaty.

I'd bowed a lot in taekwondo, but this was my first official theater bow. We practiced curtain call at dress rehearsal but we didn't actually bow. It was another one of

Mrs. Delany's superstitions. "A show isn't complete without an audience," she explained.

But, boy, was there an audience now! And everyone was cheering and clapping and snapping pictures.

After everyone took their turns, including the crew, the curtain closed.

I couldn't wait to do it all over again the next day.

Backstage, we hugged and complimented each other's performances until Mrs. Delany called for us to arc up. "Bravo, friends!" She beamed. "I loved the energy and positivity. Your hard work showed. Yes, there were a few rough spots, but the important thing is we pulled through.

"And, ensemble." Here Mrs. Delany paused and clasped her hands together. "Favorite. Save. Ever!"

She went around to everyone who'd been onstage when things went wonky and gave them high fives. When she got to me, she put up both hands.

"You get a high ten," she said, and winked. Leaning in, she added, "A star knows how to help others shine."

Wait. Did Mrs. Delany just call me *a star?*

After I hung up my costumes in the dressing room, I headed down the hallway. It was blocked off, so only the cast and crew were there, and parent volunteers. We were supposed to meet our families in the lobby.

"Hey, Eliza!" JJ called.

I turned around and waited for him to catch up.

"Nice job tonight!" he said. "That was good thinking.

About the scene thing, I mean." He'd already told me this backstage, but it was nice of him to say it again.

"Thanks! I really liked your ad-lib," I told him.

He twirled his imaginary pig-stache, which cracked me up. "I think I have an excellent shot at the title this year," he deadpanned.

He didn't seem to know what to do with his hands after that. Or his feet. He started shuffling them.

"I, um, have something for you," he said.

"Yeah?" I wondered if I'd forgotten or dropped something.

He reached into his jacket and pulled out a box "Here. Sorry the bow got smooshed."

The box wasn't wrapped, so I could see what it was right away. A package of mechanical pencils.

I was confused. "Thanks," I said.

"They had yellow ones, but I liked the colored ones better. Plus, that way you can pick out your favorite color. Or whatever."

"Thanks," I said again.

JJ shoved his fidgeting hands into his pockets and looked down at the ground. "You're welcome. I saw them at the grocery store and figured they might be nice since you don't like dull pencils. This way, if the lead breaks, all you gotta do is push the button on top and fresh lead comes out."

"You're right," I said. "I hate dull pencils. But how did you know that?"

JJ looked up. "I remembered it from that time at rehearsal when you had to use the pencil sharpener backstage."

"Oh yeah! Wait. That was like forever ago," I said.

He shrugged. "I pay attention is all."

I wondered if he meant he paid attention to everyone and everything all the time. But I didn't want to ask and find out. If it was an all-the-time thing, that meant I wasn't special. Maybe he *liked liked* me and maybe he didn't. Was this "the sign"? If it was, how come I didn't know? Grass stains! This stuff was confusing.

All I knew was that I liked being around JJ and he seemed to like being around me. That was good enough.

"The pencils are awesome," I told him. "I can't wait to use them."

JJ grinned. "So. Everyone is heading over to the ice cream shop down the street. Are you going?"

"Probably," I said. "I'll have to ask my parents first."

"Cool. I'll save you a seat," JJ said. "If that's okay."

I smiled and told him it was.

WATER

I made my way through the crowds outside the cafeteria. I was looking for my parents and not really paying attention to where I was going, so I was startled when a group of boys stepped in front of me. I skidded to a stop. There were four of them, and if I'd been going just a little faster, I would have smacked right into the tallest one.

"Look. It's Nimmm-bus," the tall guy said, and sneered. "Nice job," he added sarcastically.

I froze. Almost running into him made me think of Sophia plowing into me. Master Kim said you could use your opponent's momentum against them. I couldn't quite get that in class. But when my partner came at me at my gold-belt test, I didn't resist. I moved when he moved and then he went past me and stumbled.

Wait! It made sense! Being like water didn't always mean ignoring your opponent or getting out of their way. Sometimes it meant moving *with* them.

Or, in this case, agreeing with them.

I looked the tall boy in the eye and smiled. "Thanks! We worked hard on the play. Glad you came to see it."

The group snickered. The leader sized me up. "I'm not complimenting you," he said. My whole body tingled with adrenaline.

"Oh. Sorry," I said. "I thought 'good job' implied something positive."

The rest of the group laughed again, but the tall boy was determined. "You're weird, you know that?" he snarled.

I nodded. "I've heard that before."

"Don't you care?" the boy asked.

I shrugged. "Weird is interesting."

Before the boy could figure out how to respond, I skirted my way around the group and floated down the hall.

This being-like-water thing might just work out.

ICE CREAM, YOU SCREAM

Mom and Dad were waiting for me by the lobby doors.

I could tell Mom wanted to run over and hug me but remembered my rule about No Mothering in Public.

"You were amazing, Eliza! Oh rules, schmules," she said when I was within arm's reach. I was in such a good mood, I let her hug me. It didn't take long for Dad to join in.

"You're a star!" Dad said after they stepped back and let me breathe. "Can I have your autograph?"

I blushed.

It turned out that several of the car-accident victims got rerouted to another hospital, so Mom got to sneak out early.

"I'm sorry I missed the first act," Mom told me. "And that I didn't have time to stop for flowers." She gave Dad a look. I guessed he was supposed to be in charge of that. Dad told her about Sam getting me flowers instead. She was shocked. But in a proud, happy way.

As the three of us headed out to the car, Dad said, "Speaking of Sam, I recorded the party scene for him to watch later."

"You weren't supposed to record the play," I told him. "Didn't you hear the announcement?"

Dad shrugged. "Hey. Like Mom said, 'rules, schmules.'"

The ice cream parlor people were prepared. Which was good, because everyone in the cast and crew and their families showed up!

"Dad and I will be over there," Mom said, handing me some money and pointing to where the grown-ups were.

I met up with Vivian and JJ and some other people from the ensemble and we got in line. A lot of other people were already sitting down with their sundaes and cones. Everyone was laughing and eating and talking and planning what to bring to the strike party the next night. Someone asked if I could make more cupcakes. I wouldn't have time, but I said I could probably get up early and make some "cast" cookies.

I'd been right. Theater was my thing now, too. I belonged.

Ice cream always made me thirsty, so I headed over to the water fountain. Paige and her parents were sitting at a nearby table. I didn't mean to eavesdrop, but Paige's mom was being loud.

"You're never going to keep landing roles if you continue

to forget lines," she said. "If you want to be a professional, act like one!"

Her dad cleared his throat. "Are you just wasting money on acting lessons and head shots?" he asked. "Because I assure you, I can think of plenty of other ways to spend it."

"Acting colleges are extremely competitive," her mom said. "If you think one commercial is going to get you in, you're sadly mistaken."

Wow. Paige was only in eighth grade, and her parents were already worried about college. And her professional career. No wonder Paige wanted to make a good impression on the high school director who came to watch opening night.

Paige caught me listening and scowled. I wiped the water off my mouth with my hand and hightailed it back to the table. A few minutes later, Paige tapped me on the shoulder. I followed her into the bathroom.

"Look," she said, leaning against the sink. "I want you to know that you didn't have to do what you did."

"You're welcome."

She snorted. "I wasn't *thanking* you. I was about to get things back on track and you messed that up, too."

"What else did I mess up?" I asked her.

"Everything!"

Paige wasn't making any sense. But I thought about how her parents had treated her. Especially her dad, who'd complained about the expensive acting lessons being a waste of money. I knew what it was like to have money be tight, but everyone made mistakes. Acting lessons weren't a waste. Did they notice what a good job she'd done during the rest of the play?

WWSCD—what would Sweet Caroline do?

No. What was *I* going to do?

"I know you would have figured it out," I told her.

She let out a gigantic sigh. "I know. I just said that," she told me.

She headed toward the door, but suddenly stopped and turned to me. "So. Are you going to audition for the spring play?" she asked.

"I'm thinking about it."

"Well, keep thinking about it," she said, and walked out.

ONE LAST THING

A little while later, the ice cream place started to empty out. The workers began wiping down tables. Mom and Dad were still in one of the corner booths, talking with Annie's moms and a few other parents. JJ and Vivian had already left. Call time was noon the next day, and it was going to be a long day, with two shows *and* strike! I gathered up my trash.

"Need a hand?" a voice said. It was Annie.

"Sure," I said with a shrug, even though I didn't need help.

She walked with me to the trash can. "What you did," she said. "Helping everyone get off the stage. That was cool."

I smiled. "Yeah. It was fun."

"I wanted to thank you," Annie said. "You know. For giving me a way to still come on."

"I just got you on," I said. "You were the one who cracked everyone up with your oversized curlers and kitten slippers. The bows were a nice touch, by the way."

"Thanks. The bows were mine from when I was little. I found them under my bed." (All I had under my bed was dust bunnies and the theater book. I'd dig it out when I got home.)

"You could've left me in the wings," Annie said.

I shrugged again. "Yeah, I guess."

"Why didn't you?"

I thought about this. "Because we're friends."

"Still?"

I thought about this, too. "Yes."

Annie looked down at her feet. "I haven't been a very good friend lately."

When I didn't disagree, she went on. "I'm sorry, Eliza. I really am. Especially about calling you a nimbus cloud and saying you ruin everything. It's not true. I think I just got caught up with everything, and then I got a big head and thought being friends with Paige would get me an in into the business. Or at least with the eighth graders. And, well, you were right. I guess I was jealous, too."

"About the extra line?" I asked.

Annie shook her head. "It wasn't the line. Well, it was. But that wasn't all of it. Acting was supposed to be *my* thing and then you turned out to be really good at it."

I opened my mouth to protest, but Annie interrupted.

"No. You're really good. You are. Especially at improv. That's *hard* and you make it look easy. And then it seemed like Mrs. Delany was always saying 'Good job' or 'Way to go, Eliza.'" Annie blew a stray hair out of her face. "It just made me sad. Do you know what it's like to never be noticed?"

I did know.

"It's okay," I told her.

"No, it's not. I was a real jerk. How can I make it up to you?"

"I bet we can think of something," I told her. "How 'bout wearing your old-lady costume out in public?"

Annie's eyes grew wide. "Um. I guess I could do that. Where—"

I laughed. "I'm just kidding."

Annie breathed a sigh of relief. "You're really good at keeping a straight face," she said. "Will you teach me how you do that someday?"

"Sure," I told her.

"So are we okay?" Annie asked. "Because I really miss you."

Half of the ice cream shop's lights turned off. And we both jumped. Then giggled.

"That's our cue, girls," Mo-mo called. "Time to get moving."

Annie and I headed toward the exit. "If you think about it," I deadpanned, "I wouldn't even have auditioned if it wasn't for you. So in a way, this is all your fault."

"Yeah. That was a good idea." Annie said. "I get those occasionally." She paused. "Maybe I should see a doctor about that."

I laughed. "See! You're good at improv, too." Annie grinned and the two of us fell into step.

"So," she said when we got outside. "Now that we're talking again, do you think you might like to come to my house for a sleepover? Not this weekend, but maybe next week? We have a lot of time to make up for."

I smiled wide. "Yeah. That sounds like fun."

ONE MORE LAST THING, OR WHAT WE DID AT OUR SLEEPOVER

Annie and I decided to start a new notebook.

"I think we should do something about theater," Annie said. "Maybe we could do a Rules to Surviving Your First Production."

"What about more of a self-help guide?" I suggested as I stretched out on Annie's bedroom floor on top of my new sleeping bag.

"Perfect," Annie said. "It needs a great name, though."

"Oooo!" I said. "And when we're done we should leave

it in one of the suitcases in the costume closet. Like that letter we found."

Annie got so excited, she knocked over our popcorn. "So other theater kids can find it! That's *brilliant*."

Even though Annie had the best handwriting, we decided each of us would take turns writing things down this time.

Annie and I decorated the cover of the new journal together. Afterward, Annie said I should have the honor of coming up with the first entry.

Eliza and Annie's Super Secret Tips to Stardom

Rule No. 1: Bring a friend—and always stick together.

GLOSSARY

In case you get confused or just want to know how to pronounce the taekwondo words in this book, here they are.

Your friend,
Eliza (gold belt)

bah ro (bah ROW): return to starting position

charyut (cha-RYUT): attention

choonbi (chun-BEE): ready position

danjun (don-JAHN): in martial arts, a space below your belly button believed to be the center of your energy or *ki*

dobok (doe-BOK): uniform

dojang (doe-JAHNG): training hall. (It means "house of discipline.")

hae sahn (hay SAHN): dismissed

jong yul (jong YUL): line up

kamsahhamida (gam-sah-hahm-mee-da): thank you

ki (KEE): life energy

kicho ee bo (ki-CHEW ee boo): basic form No. 2 (*Ee* means "second.")

kicho il bo (ki-CHEW ill boo): basic form No. 1 (*Il* means "first.")

kihap (KEE-hahp): spirit yell

koomahn (khoo-MAHN): stop

kyoonyae (kyoon-YEY): bow

mejoomuk (mage-MAHK): hammer fist

poomsae (poom-SAY]): form

sabumnim (SAH-bahm-nim): master instructor

seoreun (sah-ROON): thirty

shijak (shee-JAHK]): begin

shool (SHOOL): rest

taekwondo (tie-KWON-doe): the South Korean art of hand and foot fighting. *Tae* means "to use the foot." *Kwon* means "to use the hand." *Do* means "art" or "way of life."

yursit (yur-SIT): stand up

HOW TO COUNT TO TWENTY
IN KOREAN

hana (HAH-na): one
dool (DOOL): two
set (SET): three
net (NET): four
dasut (DAS-it): five
yasut (YAS-it): six
ilgop (ill-GOP): seven
yuldol (yul-DOL): eight
ahop (AH-hop): nine
yul (YOOL): ten
yul hana (YOOL HAH-na): eleven
yul dool (YOOL DOOL): twelve
yul set (YOOL SET): thirteen
yul net (YOOL NET): fourteen
yul dasut (YOOL DAS-it): fifteen
yul yasut (YOOL YAS-it): sixteen
yul ilgop (YOOL ill-GOP): seventeen
yul yuldol (YOOL yul-DOL): eighteen
yul ahop (YOOL AH-hop): nineteen
seumul (SAH-mul): twenty

ACKNOWLEDGMENTS

Writing a book, like putting on a play, requires a large cast and crew. I'd like to thank some of my fellow ensemble members here.

First, to my readers, and to the teachers and the librarians who connect them to stories: Books, like plays, aren't complete without an audience. Thank you for coming to the show.

I'd also like to thank all the amazing folks at Holiday House, who love what they do and do it so well—especially Sally Morgridge, for being the kind of editor who leaves comments like "I love this!" and "Yay!" in the margins of my manuscripts. I'm so glad you were with me on this journey once again.

To my agent extraordinaire, Marie Lamba, who gives good Christmas cards as well as advice, and who holds my hand when I freak out: you rock.

For Karen Donnelly, who brought Eliza to life on the cover: a huge thank you.

To my mom (who bought me all the books I could read when I was little), and to my dad (my first editor): my heart is full.

Thank you also to my writing friends, including anyone who has ever commiserated, answered a question, talked to me at a conference, or clicked "Like" when I shared good news or tweeted about my books. I'd like to especially thank my critique partners, Christina Farley, Susan Laidlaw, Andrea Mack, Debbie Ridpath Ohi, and Kate Fall, who are way better writers than I am and who will probably realize this any day now and still not ditch me.

Thanks to Tami Furlong, my friend and owner of Fundamentals Children's Books, Toys, and Games in Delaware, Ohio, who lets me sit on the floor of her back room and raid her boxes of ARCs. And to all of the other independent bookstore owners who go out of their way to support their local authors: we writers love you! (P.S. Happy retirement, Sally Oddi, and good luck with the new store, Melia Wolf!)

To my *dojang* family: *kamsahhamida.*

To my boys, Jim, Matt, and Sam: thank you for hand-selling my books, listening or at least pretending to listen when I talk about writing, and retrieving things on high shelves.

And finally to my daughter: Abbey, life gave you one heck of a plot twist. I know leaving your chosen path and coming home was not what you wanted. But your courage and grace inspire me daily. And this book wouldn't have been possible without you. Thank you for all the times I pestered you with questions about theater or what Eliza would say and you responded thoughtfully. I'm grateful. I'm also grateful for all the times I asked you something and you rolled your eyes or growled at me—because it meant you were still here.